Шunamängaz

Taming The Impostor Saga Book iii

Adventure Time Travel Fantasy Series
For the young at heart.

Sheri Vie

Doctor Vie Publications

Illuᴎɑmᴧᴎɠɑz version 1.0

Especially for You

Want to learn about the African setting for the series?
Go to <u>DrVie.com/Taming-The-Impostor-map</u>

✽ ✽ ✽ ✽ ✽ ✽

SHORT STORY GIFT FOR YOU
UTOPIAN ZOOKA
<u>DrVie.com/VIPfreebooks</u>
Prequel to Taming The Impostor Saga

✽ ✽ ✽ ✽ ✽ ✽

ႮⱳⱧⱨⱳⱨⱨ dedication

Honors my dearest **Mom**, who supports and accompanies me on many of the "back-routes" featured in Taming the Impostor Saga.

✧✧✧

And in reverence to:

The memory of my dearest **Dad,** who piqued my love for adventure, which catalyzed the characters,

and to

the memory of my dearest **Grandma**, and her fascinating stories of superpowers and Utopian legends, sprinkled throughout the Saga.

✧✧✧

And recently

In memory of my dear friend **Michael-Sean O'Connell**, passed at age 29 on 7 January 2017, who at my side in 2016, encountered a young boy in South Africa, who inspired the character of Siya

CONTENTS

CHAPTER ONE

Best Friends Forever

Day Three Continued

A SMILE SWEPT UP Jali's cheeks—to the corners of his green eyes, past his pointed ears—and tickled Brelize, who peered from the Earth-boy hood. The shimmering, and yet to be identified object in the palm of the young alien's hand, appeared to also captivate his squlrrel friend.

Jali inspected the smooth contraption and found nothing remarkable underneath. But the gleaming side, ooka, it promised a spectacular revelation. Tilting his newly acquired boon in the air, he squinted in the summer sunshine piercing through the bubble leaves drooping like water balloons off the black umnukane trees.

In the narrow route ahead, Kriaka sat alone inside the parked truck, silent and motionless, seemingly oblivious to his overwhelming curiosity toward her unexpected offering.

Around him, Shiana bounded. Her voice laced with girlish excitement, intensified the sparkle in her blue eyes.

"A-a mirror." She skipped faster.

"Mirror?"

The teen jutted her head over his shoulder, sending Brelize scurrying down his arm, as she jabbed her finger at their newly acquired trinket. "Yessss!"

Jali looked closer and gasped at the image lodged inside the charm. *How disconcerting! Is the star shrinking into this object the Earth beings call a mirror?* Deeply concerned about the bizarre action of the Earth's solar system, he surveyed the patches of sky peeking through the treetops, and to his delight found the planet's bright sun glowing loyally above them.

Sighing with relief, he stretched his slender finger, and tentatively touched the mini star within the mirror.

Beside him, Shiana laughed, apparently amused by his ignorance, motivating him even further to solve the mystery.

The young prince drew in a quick breath. *Ooka, of course!* "That is where the sun does not really shine, Shiana."

Through the summer forest, slivers of sunshine laced tresses of the girl's golden hair, and she glowed like a million stars as she reached for his hand, and roped him into a dance on the sandy forest patch, in the valley of the Draco Mountains.

When their frolicking simmered low, they plonked against a stinkwood trunk and Jali pondered on how to utilize his newly acquired discovery for his crucial purpose. *I must confirm a few fundamental truths before embarking further.*

He positioned the mirror near his face, and reeled back in alarm. "That's me, Prince Jali."

Shiana giggled. "T-that's you."

She grabbed the mirror and lifted it to her fair face. "H-hello, Shiana."

The young prince finally understood. The mirror resembled reflections in the Royal Garden pond on Planet Zooka, but even better, with this earthly object he could move the reflective surface wherever he wished.

Without a moment to lose, his Third Eye fluttered and scanned the convoy of parked trucks, spiny shrubs, and tree trunks, and even though there was no sign of his lost Zookian friend, he nodded. Tuttles is here. *My friend, you need me to make you visible.*

Like a sleuth on a hot trail, he tilted the mirror toward the front of Rama's truck. Jen duplicated with Kriaka in the passenger seat, validating his hypothesis. Now for the ultimate test. He angled the mirror around himself. As expected, the convoy of tribal trucks and warriors reflected in the mirror; the compact bushes and humongous trees appeared in the mirror.

But, what was that?

With a minor tweak, he repositioned the gadget to a mysterious spot between the wooded protea shrubs alongside the vehicles.

His heart pounded hard against his ribs. "Tuttles!"

The young Zookian sprinted toward the tribal warriors, who startled and bowed as he passed. In his haste, Brelize toppled off his shoulder, but he continued, racing past the trucks and pushing his way through the blades of bushes around him.

Rama's voice rang from behind. "Prince Jali!"

Distressed yells from Shiana, Majestic One, and the tribal warriors resonated through the forest, but he persisted, searching frantically deep in the spiral aloe shrubs for his friend. "Tuttles, Tuttles, Tuttles?"

The Zookian reptilian was nowhere. In vain, Jali sank to the ground and felt as if his heart would burst. *Why is this happening?* Tears blurred his vision as he struggled to discern Rama who had skidded to a halt beside him.

"Tuttles." Sobs wrenched his body.

The austere leader of the First Ones drew him close and hugged his trembling body. Time stood still as the utopian prince nestled in the rhythmic beats of Rama's strong heart. When his sobs quieted, he received a kiss on his head, and they rose.

Brelize, the tribal warriors, Shiana, and Majestic One encircled the pair, and their eyes glistened.

Without a hint of warning a shrill echo rented the air. The troops screamed and ducked; their hands shielding their heads.

High in the African sky, something foreign circled and swooped into the trees. It darted through the branches toward them, trailing a high-pitched whistle, following them as they ran farther into the forest.

Rama pushed Jali to the ground. "Duck!"

The hiss bypassed them and Jali breathed easier. But as the airborne shriek changed direction and headed directly for them, his relief dissipated and his pointed ears shut tight.

A thunderous boom shuddered the ground close to them, and their screams filled the forest once more.

Jali's ears perked, as sweat dripped down his face. Edging out from Rama's protection, he squinted through the settling dust and his heart skipped a beat.

"Tuttles!" With a leap, he reached the colossal emerald carapace of the four-legged Zookian.

"Your Highness, what took you so long?" Tuttles' blue tongued licked dry the prince's face.

"Tuttles, I love you, Tuttles." Jali clung onto the reptile, afraid to let go. For the first time since his three days on planet Earth, a surge of hope flowed through his small frame.

Shiana already at their side, yelped with joy. But the tribal warriors appeared terrified as they cowered on their knees. Alongside them, Rama and Majestic One stared with their mouths agape.

"Tuttles, where have you been, my friend?"

"Your Highness, I have been with you all along. You ignored me! What a strange place. Nobody talks to the animals or the plants or trees."

Shiana's laughter broke the tension around them, and the warriors rose, but kept their gazes lowered.

"Tuttles, we are indebted to my Earth friend Shiana, who rallied her creatures to find you," Jali said.

The young girl blushed and curtsied.

Jali's Third Eye fluttered and scanned his friend's shell. What was peculiar about the reptile? "Tuttles, what have you been eating? Have you fattened?"

The creature floated above Jali. He extended his leathery, rugged limbs, and squirmed. "Well, as luck may have it, I have also befriended an Earth creature."

Tuttles inserted his claw deep into his shell and pulled out a furry, sandy ball. It unwound and leapt down.

"Meosic!" Shiana ran to her. The sand cat they believed had been killed sprang into the girl's arms, stretched her neck and meowed. Her yellow-green eyes twinkled in her broad flat head.

Jali felt overjoyed with the double celebration; both he and Shiana were finally reunited with their dearest friends.

Yet a hollowness deep within him surfaced. Someone was absent from their jubilation. Narrowing his gaze, he searched for the enchanting face which had solved the mystery and wrapped them with happiness. But she was not there. He pouted and threaded his way through the cheery group toward Jen.

Inside the truck, Kriaka remained rigid, staring ahead. He gently pried open the rusty door and bowed.

"Kriaka Adi, you led me to Tuttles."

She sat motionless.

Overwhelmed with gratitude he rested his head on her chest, where her heart beat shallow.

Tuttles emerged from the thicket and hovered by his side.

"Kriaka Adi, I have the pleasure to introduce you to my dear turtle friend, Tuttles." Jali placed her hand on the creature's mosaic shell. "Tuttles, meet the esteemed leader of the pure beings, the First One, Kriaka Adi."

"Pleased to meet you, leader of the pure beings, Kriaka Adi. You are very beautiful."

Jali gasped; Kriaka's hand had become invisible. His

Third Eye fluttered, but before he could make sense of the incident, Shiana, Rama, Magnificent One, and the tribal warriors had reached them. He quickly removed her hand as the team gathered around Jen. Their eyes shone with hope, their bodies readied for success. But Kriaka did not move, and their faces grew long.

A feeling of nervousness dampened Jali's spirits. What if Kriaka Adi did not regain her memory before they reached the Portal?

His heart pounded. *I must be a gallant Zookian.* He pushed his slender chest out as far as he could, and spoke with an air of confidence. "Kriaka Adi and Rama Adi, Tuttles and I shall join Michael and Siya to assist in the location of the stolen GIFT. Thereafter we shall rendezvous with you at the Mont Aux Sources base camp."

Rama raised his eyebrows and tightened his cap in the manner in which Jali had become accustomed to.

Sensing his trepidation, he continued. "Rama Adi, it will be the first time I shall leave your protection, but I shall be safe with Tuttles. We realize the future of the pure beings and your planet rests with Kriaka Adi, and we are determined to help ignite her memory."

Rama frowned and paced.

But Jali continued. "Kriaka Adi, we shall return with the information you seek." He kissed her unresponsive hands and bowed.

✳ ✳ ✳ ✳ ✳ ✳

CHAPTER TWO

First Superhero Mission

The thought of his first Earth adventure with Tuttles excited Jali. He could finally be of help to his intergalactic friends and simultaneously restore his grandma's health.

Meosic, with Brelize perched atop her sandy brown back, purred at his side.

"Watch over Kriaka and Shiana, my friends."

He heaved himself on Tuttles and beamed with delight. What an incredible feeling to be once more on his friend's carapace. *I am ready for my first flight on planet Earth.* Tuttles rose and hovered above the wide-eyed troops, as Jali waved, before his Third Eye fluttered and they became invisible.

Below them, Shiana, Majestic One, Rama, and the tribal warriors watched with looks of amazement. *Could*

333

333

333

it be? Ooka, Kriaka Adi waved from the truck.

Enthused, he draped his body on the familiar Zookian shell and rested his face on his friend's rippled neck. "Tuttles I am thankful to have you with me again!"

"But Your Highness, I have been at your beckoning all the time. I hoped you would release me from the invisible knot sooner."

"My friend, if Shiana had not relayed messages to Earth's creatures and Kriaka had not solved the mysterious rhyme, you would still be in tangles. I dread to think what could have happened." He hugged his friend and kissed his thick neck. "I hope Kriaka heals in time to open the Portal."

"Your Highness, prioritize. We must first prove worthy and contribute to Michael and Siya's undertaking. Hold on tight, for your first ride on planet Earth."

They ascended past glossy green stinkwood leaves and over the treetops.

The scenery below took Jali's breath away. They rose above the lush canopy of forests, sheltered between lofty mountain ridges glowing fiery red in the summer blaze. The valley teamed with creatures, big and small, some of whom had become familiar to him.

This planet revealed a similar terrain to their blissful Zooka. The smell of yellowwood cones, the chirps of birds, the waves of cool breeze, the taste of raindrops, and

11

many of the natural wonders he encountered here reminded him of home.

He needed to return to Zooble and reestablish contact with Grandma. *I cannot lose her too.* Anxiety clawed at his heart, and he closed his eyes. The memory of her scent of roses calmed the palpitations, as they always did.

With ripened confidence, he once more flew on his trusted companion, making Reena's birthday party seem like Z-years past. Much had happened since, and he missed Brela and his friends dreadfully.

"Tuttles, what have you surmised about planet Earth? Why does it resonate familiar features to Zooka?"

The creature buzzed. "Your Highness, from my Tut Senses, the flora and fauna are ninety-eight percent similar to Zooka."

Ooka; the atmosphere from high up here continued to embrace them.

A crowned eagle swooped close to the invisible pair, and Tuttles veered to the right.

"Your Highness, unfortunately, ninety percent of the human species vibrate at less evolved levels. Although their brain sizes are larger than most other beings, their super conscious capacities appear underdeveloped. Luckily for you and I, we were rescued by those with enhanced consciousness, and who oscillate stronger energy fields."

Tuttles boasted with his notorious three-sixty-degree turn and Jali clung close.

"Your Highness, I encountered several petite reptiles, including a dwarf chameleon, and discovered that I am the only reptilian species here who flies!"

Jali chuckled, before his ears perked and his Third Eye fluttered. "Tuttles, I sense an SOS!"

They decelerated and coasted. In the grassland below, in the river winding alongside the mountain, tribal children played. Upstream, females balanced buckets of water on their heads, and downstream a smaller group washed clothing at the riverbank. In the nearby village, outside their huts, elders watched.

In an instant, the tranquil scene tore asunder, as an open truck sped across the oat grass and screeched to a stop, across a gathering of children frolicking under a monkey-thorn tree beside the stream. Four broad-shouldered Dragons grabbed a child each, and hastened to their vehicle.

Jali flinched. "They are stealing the children."

"Your Highness, I think it is time for a rescue mission."

Tuttles flew low over the river and clamped his white claws onto several boulders.

"I shall attack the Dragons, Your Highness. You

steady yourself."

They loomed over the escaping Dragons, and dropped the boulders around them. Screams ripped the air, and as the Dragons released the children, Tuttles whisked them to safety.

"Aikona!" the Dragons shouted, before jumping into the truck and fleeing in a blaze of dust. Behind them the tribal folk looked to the sky and bowed their heads.

Jali waved excitedly before he remembered. "They cannot see us."

"All the better, Your Highness!"

"Hayibo."

"Hayibo," Tuttles replied. "Our mission is incomplete!"

They hovered over the getaway truck, and Jali's ears perked, tuning in to the conversation.

"Aikona, the Spirits are after us," one Dragon said.

"Now we have no captives for the traffickers! What do we tell them?"

The driver moaned. "They'll never believe the flying rocks and those flying children!"

"I don't want to be doing this again. My mother, she told me the one in the sky is watching, now I know!" One of the two Dragons in the rear of the truck sounded distressed.

Jali chortled, and his mischievous streak ignited.

"Tuttles, are you thinking what I am?"

"Why not, Your Highness? Why not, I say?"

Jali positioned himself to the back side of the shell and pinned his legs tight around his friend's hind leg. "I want my share of the fun too."

They flew low over the stream and paused as Jali reached down and collected handfuls of stones.

He crinkled his nostrils and curled his upper lip in disgust. "Oh, Tuttles, you farped. That odor is awful."

"My apologies, Your Highness, the edibles on this planet upset my tender constitution. That farp was a long time in the coming. Do I smell okay now?"

Jali groaned and twisted his mouth as the putrid smell lifted. "Ooka." Spinning forward he adjusted himself. "Let the fun commence."

They raced to the rear of the vehicle, where two of the Dragons clutched long rifles and glued their gazes to the sky.

With the pebbles, Jali pelted the Dragon on the left.

He glared at the one beside him. "Hayibo, wenzani?"

"Mina? Ay, lutho. I'm not doing anything."

The Dragon shook his head, and with a look of confusion resumed his position as the truck bounced along the dirt road.

Jali was not done yet. Stifling his giggle, he showered his victim with more pebbles.

"Mina uyo shaya wena!" the Dragon shouted.

"What are you saying? I didn't do anything! Why you want to hit me?"

The superheroes hovered closer, and Tuttles released a boulder in the gap between them.

"Hayibo!" they shouted, and leapt out from the moving truck.

"Hayibo!" Jali shouted.

"Hayibo!" Tuttles shouted, in his thick base voice.

The driver screeched to a halt and poked his head out of the window. "What's wrong?"

"Hay, the Spirits are mad with us!" the Dragons shouted.

Tuttles dropped his last boulder onto the front of the truck. The Dragons screamed and jumped out, joining their mates already on their knees.

"You have angered the Spirits by stealing children and trafficking them," Tuttles boomed in Zulu. "If you do not pledge to stop now, I shall change you into rats."

"Aikona, noooo. Noooooo. I stop. Promise." The kidnappers appeared terrified. They bowed their heads and repeated their promises.

Tuttles twisted his lanky neck and winked at Jali before continuing in a thunderous voice. "Promises are insufficient. You must repent by serving the tribal village, where you will be kind, helpful, and hardworking."

"Yes, Spirit, I promise!"

Tuttles boomed even louder. "Go now! I am watching you, wherever you are."

Jali flung the remaining pebbles at their feet.

"I promise, I promise." The four ran back to the village, closely followed by the invisible superheroes.

"We're sorry, no more, no more bad stuff. We help you now, we become your friends." The Dragons clasped the feet of the elders and stretched face down. Around them the children, villagers, and elders scanned the sky and applauded.

Jali felt overjoyed.

"Mission one accomplished, Your Highness!" Tuttles brushed his neck onto Jali's face and laughed. "I like our superhero mission!"

"Yebo."

"Yebo."

The pair departed at Zarp-speed to Spioenkop.

✳ ✳ ✳ ✳ ✳ ✳

CHAPTER THREE

Spy Hill

Energized by their first rescue mission, the superheroes flew over stretches of grasslands nestled in the lower plains of the Draco Mountains, and followed the trickle of river east toward Spioenkop. Jali reveled at the changing landscape as they soared.

Back on Zooka, his newly acquired ability to fly on Tuttles restricted them to low altitudes, but here on planet Earth they mounted to new heights.

"Why is it we can fly higher here, Tuttles?"

"I am unable to provide a worthy answer, Your Highness, but I am enjoying our enhanced superpowers."

Soon, the grasslands switched to parched expanses of land, and a strange swell surged to Jali. His Third Eye fluttered, and he caught his breath. "I am sensing undesirable vibrations."

The reptilian buzzed. "We are southwest of a town called Ladysmith, Your Highness. Planet Earth's chronology reveals humans called the British, and their allies from the countries known as Canada, Australia, and New Zealand raged a civil war against the Boers occupying South Africa, between 1899 and 1902. The fighting massacred twenty-two thousand soldiers, but also forty-four thousand innocent women, children and local tribal people under dreadful circumstances.

"The Second Boer War was won by the Boers, here at Spioenkop, the Spy Hill you see below us. Sixty years passed, and the area converted into a nature reserve. Since the Dark Period fifty years back, rumors declared Spioenkop to be haunted."

"Haunted?"

"Ooka, Your Highness. Unexplained nocturnal scenes, screams, and sightings have been documented. Occupants evacuated the region and barricaded the main access routes."

The desolate trail below showed no evidence of habitation, except for a hill under a dense cover of rubble, gray rocks and stones.

"Look, the two tribal trucks." Jali pointed. On one side of the mount, tribal warriors guarded a tall, tapered opening, the tight web of their spearheads barricaded the lower third of the entrance, and their shields blockaded

19

the floor.

"Prepare yourself, Your Highness."

Jali flattened himself on the shell, and they floated unnoticed past the tops of the pointed spears at crawl speed, continuing in slow motion through a dimly lit narrow stone tunnel.

"I hear Michael and Siya."

"Ooka, Your Highness, they are close."

He tuned his hearing in to a series of rhythmic clicks.

Tuttles buzzed. "Your Highness, they are accessing the artificial computer frame, it attempts to mimic our super consciousness. This planet called it the Accumulated Intelligence Core, AIC, an archaic method of unveiling information. It strives to accomplish what I excel at, Your Highness."

Jali recalled Michael's reference to the AIC at the tribal village. " I postulate that Michael and Siya are requesting the AIC to retrieve archived records about the GIFT."

While the pair hovered in a spacious vestibule gutted with three tunnel entrances, the clicking stopped and rushed footsteps echoed from the far right. Siya and Michael emerged, each clutching a device close to their chests.

"Hello, Siya." Jali greeted the earthling.

Siya and Michael halted, and glared in the direction

of Jali's voice.

Michael wielded a short blue cylindrical weapon in one hand. "Show yourself, or I'll shoot!" Siya backed up against him.

"Michael, it is me, Prince Jali."

"Jali or Bali, I don't care. I have one of the most dangerous weapons yet invented. One shot and you'll evaporate into specks of dust."

Tuttles whispered. "They cannot see us, Your Highness."

With haste, the duo landed, and Jali descended. His Third Eye fluttered, and gradually, from his feet to his head, he rendered himself visible.

At the full sight of Jali, Michael's hand trembled, and he lowered the weapon.

"Aikona." Siya rocked his body and head, in a manner already familiar to Jali. "The Spirits are on us!"

"Siya, it is me, Shiana's friend, remember my sister, Princess Reena and Grandma?"

"Prince, hayibo, it's you. Hay how?"

"Yebo," Jali said.

Siya lowered the device and instinctively hugged him, before disengaging and bowing.

"Wow!" Michael's tone hinted nervousness.

Siya looked around and behind Jali. "Prince, who were you talking to?"

"I found Tuttles with the help of Shiana and Kriaka Adi."

"Tuttles is here! Where, Prince?" The boy's black eyes widened.

Amid static and fizz Tuttles uncloaked his formidable emerald shell and floated over Jali.

Michael sank to his knees.

"Hayibo, hayibo." Siya bopped in to his tribal dance.

Tuttles landed and grinned. "Pleased to meet you, Siya. Pleased to meet you, Michael."

Jali, unable to contain his curiosity, pushed his way forward. "You know where the GIFT is?"

But before they could reply, his ears perked, and his Third Eye fluttered. "We must leave, now!" he shouted.

The tunnel rumbled. Tuttles flew out and back in again. "Dragon trucks will arrive in two Earth minutes, Your Highness."

Jali hopped onto his shell, and under their cloaks of invisibility they flew ahead of the earthlings. Outside, the trucks revved as Siya and Michael leaped in, followed by the warriors, and the vehicles stormed from the hill.

Jali and Tuttles landed atop the roof of the open lead truck.

"I suggest we stay invisible until I introduce you to the tribal warriors."

"Excellent idea, Your Highness." Tuttles chuckled.

"This is an easy way to travel. Though too bumpy for me."

Jali pinched his nostrils. "Tuttles!"

The tribal warriors wrinkled their nostrils and glared suspiciously at each other.

"Oh, dear me, I apologize, Your Highness. I shall not chew on those red berries again. I deduce it to be the last farp."

Jali held his nose tight.

"Is it gone, Your Highness?"

He reluctantly released one nostril. "Ooka."

"Oh Tuttles, I am delighted you are with me, farps and all."

His devoted friend grinned, and retreated his head into his carapace.

Jali remembered the devices Siya and Michael had carried out of Spioenkop. "Michael has the location of the GIFT. The good news will recharge Kriaka's spirit." With no response forthcoming, he prompted. "Well Tuttles?"

The creature's long neck slid out, and his head bopped. "I hope you are correct, Your Highness." His neck brushed on Jali. "You do know you impressed Guardian 1 when you extracted the bullet from Doctor Herby, and when you used your Third Eye to release Kriaka from the cage and Rama from the chains?"

Jali sighed and bit his lower lip. "I wish I could have

saved Doctor Herby. I am still to understand what Reena meant about us not changing history?"

"A thousand years has much in the making, Your Highness."

Jali strained his neck, and felt even more confused. "What does the reference to time mean?"

"Our Magnificent ZW7 warriors have not killed any being on any mission, Your Highness. Their role is to support the locals and to rectify only what has been changed by the Dark Force."

"By the Impostor?"

"Ooka, the Impostor. Once you graduate to Level 5, you will be privy to the history of Force Two and its hold over the Cosmos."

To their right, steep sandstone ramparts rose into arched pillars of jagged rock as they drove to rendezvous with the troops. From where Jali sat, the soaring buttresses of the rugged Draco mountain captured his attention. Wherever he looked, a nurturing ancient power welcomed him, seemingly devoid of the Impostor. He wondered why Force Two would want to inflict harm on such serene and calming beings.

"Now, Your Highness, as I was saying, before you so rudely interrupted me..."

Jali chortled. "Tuttles, where did you learn to talk in this manner?"

"You see what happens when you desert me? I learned from close imitation of the Earth—"

Jali's ears perked, and his heart raced. *Something is wrong!*

* * * * * *

CHAPTER FOUR

Poachers Corner

Tuttles buzzed. "You are hearing poachers in the nature reserve! Hold on, Your Highness."

They zoomed southeast toward the distress signals, and over a row of abandoned dwellings. "Are these poachers?"

"They are yet to come. What you see Your Highness, are called hotels, constructed by the humans for travelers to rest and recharge. See the one to our right, that was Mont Aux Sources Hotel and to the left are the remains of extravagant huts, called chalets."

At the mention of Mont Aux Sources, Jali's heart thumped. He wished that the devices carried by Michael and Siya will recover Kriaka. That a storm of sadness reached out from the desolate area below, concerned him. *Why is this planet inundated with sorrow?*

"Your Highness, the accommodation was abandoned since the Dark Period, and is now infested with poachers from the neighboring Basotho Land.

"What are poachers?"

"You are soon to experience them personally, Your Highness."

They passed a short forest and entered a field of rolling grass, where a deafening rumble ushered them in. Below, a herd of eland antelopes raced across the grassland, followed by truck loads of men, aiming long barreled weapons atop wheels.

"Poachers! We must stop them."

"On your command, Your Highness."

"Tuttles, rocks cannot help us this time."

"I fear not."

Jali had an idea, and wondered if it would work. "We switch antelopes for rocks?"

"We may be too late Your Highness!"

Below them the elands were unknowingly running toward a steep ravine, to their deaths.

On the opposite cliff, a short distance from the edge of the ravine a pride of forty young white lions together with an elder lion couple, watched.

"We can summon their help?"

"We can try, Your Highness."

They landed next to the majestic couple and unveiled

themselves. The elders appeared unperturbed by their unannounced visitors.

Jali bowed. "King Lion, Queen Lion, I am Prince Jali of Zooka."

Queen Lion nodded. "We received word you would be in our region soon, Prince Jali."

He bowed lower. "We need your help to prevent the elands from falling to their deaths."

"There are too many of them, and the poachers are too close behind. What can we do from this side of the mountain?"

Jali's Third Eye fluttered. "We can take care of the poachers, but we need your help to rally your herd of lions to steer the eland off their tragic path."

King Lion's strong body rippled in the afternoon sun, and his thick white mane flowed behind. He raised his head to the young lions and roared above the echoes of the racing elands.

The pride roared in turn, successfully catching the attention of the elands nearing the edge of the ravine. The herd turned and continued to flee along the cliff, narrowly escaping death. But their plight quickly worsened.

Gunshots and dust crammed the air, as the poachers in hot pursuit narrowed the gap between their vehicles and the racing antelopes.

"King Lion and Queen Lion, we can stop the poachers, with your help, if you fly with us." Jali said.

The pair roared. "How can we old ones refuse the chance to fly? It is our dream come true! Ready when you are, Prince Jali."

Tuttles hoisted the majestic beasts firm within each of his fore claws, and they flew across the ravine toward the poachers.

At the sight of the flying lions, the lead truck skidded to a halt.

"Aikona!" the poachers screamed.

Tuttles commanded in Xhosa. "You have angered the Spirits by entering our animal kingdom. We will destroy your manliness as punishment."

"Let's shoot them!" One of the poachers took aim at the lions.

"Oh, we are doomed," Queen Lion said. "At least we die flying."

Jali's Third Eye fluttered. He focused his energy between his eyebrows and a recognizable warmth rush through his body, as his Third Eye opened, projecting a laser beam, setting the tires of the vehicle ablaze. Amid terrifying screams, the men jumped off the trucks and knelt in obedience.

Jali shivered and he felt limp as he clung onto Tuttles.

"Hold on, Your Highness. I am not finished." The

Zookian creature dangled the lions closer to their captives. "You have angered the Spirits of the Basotho Land. You will be spared if you pledge to never bother the kingdom again."

"I promise, Great One, I promise." The group ran across the field and disappeared into the dense forest.

Tuttles paused over the entourage of elands safely gathered in the adjacent woodlands, before returning the lions to their pasture.

Jali tottered off Tuttles, and even though not fully recuperated, he was intent on appeasing his piqued curiosity. "Queen Lion, King Lion, how did you predict our arrival?"

"Prince Jali, we learned that you instructed the founding pure beings at the cave in Giant's Castle, yet many creatures were skeptical of the messengers, until Shiana's pleas verified your call. Now the hope for peace is spreading quickly around the land, and many are preparing to support you at Mont Aux Sources," Queen Lion said.

The good news sparked a surge of energy through Jali. Fully rejuvenated, he mounted Tuttles, and thanked King Lion and Queen Lion before taking leave.

Once airborne, he pondered the words of the lions. *A key mystery may be solved.*

"Look, Your Highness, the tribal trucks are reaching

the entrance of the nature reserve."

They flew ahead, eager to apprise Kriaka and the troops with news of Spioenkop, and stealthily passed multitudes of vehicles and tribal warriors, before deactivating their invisible shield.

Shiana's shrieks of delight were the first to welcome them as they landed by Rama. Next to him, Kriaka smiled and Jali's heart skipped a beat. *Perhaps she is recovered.*

"Siya and Michael will arrive soon, Kriaka Adi."

Her hazel brown eyes twinkled and he felt ecstatic. Their mission was successful. He would soon be back on Zooble.

Cheerful shouts heralded the arrival of the envoy, and the camp buzzed with excitement. Majestic One announced that the treks up Mont Aux Sources would begin at the break of dawn, and he commanded the troops to set up the campsite before nightfall.

Warriors rushed to and fro, intent on their tasks, as Jali watched in awe, with his friend Brelize comfortably nestled at her favorite spot in his Earth-boy hood.

❋ ❋ ❋ ❋ ❋ ❋

CHAPTER FIVE

The Confession

Michael raised one end of the tent pole, opposite Rama, and pulled it taut. He hammered a peg into the ground and chatted with the troops around him. They didn't seem to be bothered about his presence.

For the first time since he could remember, diverse colors, races, ages, genders, and cultures worked side by side in compassionate unity, devoid of competition. The warriors smiled at each other, *and* at him. Focused, motivated, and enthused—their moods a startling contrast to the pessimistic vibrations of the Dragons he was raised with.

After assembling the main tent and the leaders' tent, he aided a group of warriors to open up a boarded well and filled pails with water.

Beside him a warrior raised a bucket and placed it on his shoulder. "Okay, bru?" the warrior asked.

Michael's blue eyes glistened. Struggling to contain his emotions, he nodded and followed the water line to the chef's zone, where he emptied the pail into one of the potjies on the crackling fire.

Outside the leaders' tent, Siya, Shiana, and Jali laid fruit, vegetables, bread, and water on rocks near the fire. At the entrance to tent, Rama spoke animatedly to Majestic One.

Kriaka's slender body stood rooted at the side of the main tent, her head turned to the sky, her gaze fixed in the distance.

Michael sighed and dug his feet into the sand. *I wish Herby was here; he'd be so thrilled.* He shuffled nervously and glanced around him. *I wonder if I should break the news to them tonight.*

With trepidation, he approached the lone figure, and for several minutes their gazes fixed on the darkening sky, until he broke the silence. "He saved my life twice, you know."

Her lovely face turned to him with the look of a frightened child.

Spurred by her response, he cleared his throat and continued. "When they stormed the castle searching for you, I was escaping from my father's clutches. Out the back door, I bumped into Herby. I think we must've startled each other, but then something caught our attentions."

She watched him, without blinking.

He swallowed hard and continued. "A shadowy figure was standing inside the hallway, aiming a gun at me. Before I knew what had happened, a shot rang out and Herby jumped in front of me. He took the bullet." He bit hard on his lower lip, trying to deflect survivor's guilt.

"You didn't shoot my Herb?"

"No, Kriaka, how could I?"

She blinked and her eyes teared.

Herby's kind face floated in his mind. "Herby saved my life once before, when I was a little boy. Long story. Remind me to tell you someday." He sighed. "Anyway, I was ten the first time I ran away from the castle. But I was so clumsy that I cut my leg on the barbed wire fence, and collapsed close to the road. A passerby took me to the children's hospital. Herby was there; he stitched my leg and stayed at my bed all through the night. I couldn't sleep, so he told me stories of the constellations and happy planets. He was an amazing man. I wished that night that he could be my father. I've always admired him from afar."

His gaze drifted to Rama. "You're lucky to have family who love you so dearly." Unable to hold back his emotions, he choked, and with drooped shoulders, trudged to the campfire slowly filling with troops.

The flames crackled, and the clear night sky twinkled with myriad of stars. To any observer, the camp appeared to be a happy weekend outing that families spoke of. *Why do I have to carry the heavy burden?*

Junior, Majestic One, and Rama joined the campfire.

"Rama, how many First One warriors are you expecting?" Majestic One's Zulu accent, sounded regal.

"About one hundred and fifty to two hundred if the word got out well." Rama craned his head and peered into the parking lot.

"Yebo, we followed your instructions. The buses were arranged in the village." The tribal leader's feathered headdress swayed.

Rama checked again. "I wonder what's taking them so long." The glow of the fire deepened the furrows on his forehead. "Man, I just hope nothing's gone down."

He sank his muscled frame on the tussock grass and caught the chef's sandwich Majestic One flung to him. "Michael, I'm so glad you escaped the Dragons at Spioenkop."

Michael indicated toward Jali and Tuttles. "We had some help!"

Rama grunted and gobbled the thick farm bread.

Michael watched him with fascination. *I'm with my father's sworn enemy!* Yet a strange aura drew him close to the rebel. *Just like men to fight over a woman.*

He recalled the striking painting of the blue-eyed beauty he hardly knew, plastered around the mansion and castle. Why did she have to die and leave him alone with the wretch of a man who hated the sight of him?

"You have her face; stay out of my sight, you hear?" His father's words rang loud in his head. If only he could shake that haunting voice inside him.

Father and son made no secret of their hatred for each other. He sighed as he looked around the swell of two hundred troops who had rallied from many tribal villages to heed the call from Majestic One. He couldn't believe the experience. He sat elbow to elbow with the man he was brainwashed to believe to be his enemy; the man his father had plotted to torture.

"Here." Rama handed him a sandwich. The man munched and gave him the thumbs-up in between mouthfuls. "Good?"

He nodded. Yes, the simple meal was surprisingly good. Opposite him, Jali bit into a spotted yellow mango. *I bet that's what they eat on Zooka.*

Rama checked the parking lot again, but there were still no buses in sight! "Michael, what did you gather from Spioenkop? I hope we now know where the GIFT is."

On the mention of the GIFT, Kriaka made her way toward them, and all ears homed in on Michael. He choked and swallowed the chunk of bread, whole.

Sitting next to the prince, Siya interrupted in the nick of time. "Hayibo, that place, that place hides many secrets. I'm happy Michael knew where to look."

"Ja, but Siya is the genius, quite the computer genius!" Michael attempted to redirect the questioning.

"All my sneaking around the schools trained this brain." Siya knocked on his head.

The camp roared with laughter, and Majestic One tugged at the boy's thick braids.

Before Michael knew it, a somber silence blanketed them, and he shot a glance at Kriaka standing behind Rama.

He knew he could no longer hide and his face heated as he cleared his throat. "Hmm. Well, we searched through the hidden electronic files but couldn't get in. Ja, then Siya broke through the password."

Another round of cheers echoed around the campfire, and in the silence that followed Rama stared intently at him.

He swallowed hard. "The thing is…" He coughed as the flames heated his already flushed face. "The thing is…" He stretched his jaw and blurted, "The GIFT may no longer be in South Africa."

A vacuum of silence sucked the crackles from the roaring fire into an abysmal pit of nothingness, as Kriaka collapsed onto Rama.

Shiana screamed and rushed to her sister's side.

Rama checked her pulse. "She's fainted." He turned and yelled, "Get her some water!" He carried her limp body to the main tent, ducked his head and disappeared, with Shiana at his heels.

Jali, Tuttles, Majestic One, and Junior piled into the main tent. Michael trailed in last. His head felt heavy.

Siya ran in with the water. "Is she okay?"

Rama took the enamel cup from the boy. "Yeah, it's been a long day. She needs to rest. Tomorrow is gonna be a hard trek." He raised her from the hammock bed and fed her like a little child. "You'll be okay, sis. Never you mind, we're gonna find out where the GIFT is, and once we get the prince to Zooble, Princess Reena and the Magnificent ZW7 warriors will retrieve the GIFT."

She nodded and turned away from them. Rama tucked her in, kissed her head, and urged the group out. Michael hovered behind.

"Shiana, get some rest with sis." Rama kissed the girl's head leaving her and Meosic with Kriaka.

The two men joined the restless group at the campfire, where the flames were leaping high.

The inevitable question emerged from Rama. "What do you mean, the GIFT may not be in South Africa?"

Michael scratched his stubbled chin and answered as best he could. "The AIC was coded to keep a track of the

GIFT." He stared hard at the dancing flames. "The only thing is, it was limited within certain boundaries."

"What the heck does that mean?" Rama shouted.

Michael rolled his tongue around his dry mouth and smacked his lips. "AIC can't track past the landmass of South Africa."

The smothering silence urged him to continue.

"When Siya activated the tracking system records for up to yesterday, we determined that the signal disappeared at the edge of the landmass in Balito. But real AIC time-tracking today shows nothing!"

The confused faces stared at him.

"The GIFT was moved out of the boundary of South Africa at precisely ten o'clock last night!"

❋ ❋ ❋ ❋ ❋ ❋

CHAPTER SIX

The Revelation

For a moment, Michael and his attentive listeners stared past the silhouette of the tremendous Amphitheater plateau in the distance, and up to the starlit African sky.

It was a beautiful still night, punctuated with the trills of bush crickets, alternating with the crackling fire and the pounding of two hundred hearts.

Rama's stunned face reflected the mood around the camp. "The GIFT was moved out of the boundaries at ten p.m. last night!" He let out an exasperated sigh, and his eyes tracked Michael. "Does Chan have the expertise to move the GIFT without detection?"

Michael grimaced. An image of his father in the bunker lab beneath the castle flashed before him and he nodded. "He's invested everything to seize the GIFT and harness its powers for his sole use."

A long-awaited question came from the prince.

"What *can* he do with the GIFT?"

Michael raised his eyebrows; striking scenes flashed before him as if they occurred yesterday. "When I was little, I recall watching my father through the garden window at the castle. He was in the library, pacing like a madman. Unkempt and unshaven, he was muttering to my grandfather's portrait about world domination and making his lost dream a reality. Something about ruling the planet."

The group stared at him, but he went on. "As I grew, I learned that he was passionately searching, with confiscated space technology, for the lost Goldilocks planet. I heard rumors that people were being sent into space as guinea pigs, to see how long they could last under inhumane conditions, but I refused to believe any of it."

Two hundred gazes locked on him as he smoothed out his drenched shirt, clinging to his chest like a safety blanket. "The project continued, with prominent leaders around the world investing money."

He stopped. He gasped. An insight.

He tugged at his lips. *Oh dear me, that's it.*

"Go on, what happened?" Rama urged.

"One day I noticed a strange man with him. After that there was such a drastic change in my father. It was as if he was possessed."

He jumped up, and stood rooted, overwhelmed by the realization that had escaped him for so many years.

"The man, the man, Michael! Who was the man?" Rama shouted.

Michael paced and narrowed his gaze. "You know, I noticed him hanging around Father, sometimes even at our castle. No one dared talk about *the man* in any way. All I remembered was the terrible fear and dread when he was around. Father worsened over time. The man, the man, his dark face, that horrible voice! Oh dear Lord, that face."

He paused and turned to the quieted crowd, his eyes wide with the revelation, his skin thick with goosebumps.

"Pierre!" He screamed and clutched his head, sinking to the sand. "Dear heavens above, that man was Pierre!"

Suddenly it seemed as if the oxygen was once again sucked out of the fire as pitch darkness enveloped the campsite, but this time paralyzing each one of them. Within a second it released them, and they gasped for air.

Michael panted and rose. He paced fast, his heart raced out of control. He yanked at his wet blond hair. "When people got suspicious of the rise in reports of missing persons, they became vigilant. That's when father sent the Dragons in the dead of night into the townships to collect people. But then there were inherent problems in transportation to Mars and the Moon. One night I overheard him mutter that he would rekindle the work on teleportation."

The prince stood and leaned on Tuttles. "Teleportation?"

Michael nodded. "One day Pierre returned, said something about recurring vibrations, and told father to deploy the drones."

Majestic One leapt to his feet. "Drones were destroyed fifty years ago, when the Dark Period started!"

Michael shook his head and tightened his lips. "Grandfather had stored the best of them before that." He nodded, the feeling of guilt overpowered him, and his voice quivered. "Ja, they had it all planned, for a long, long time!"

Rama leaned forward and whispered, "Where were the vibrations coming from?"

Michael wiped his forehead and edged close to him. His voice thickened. "Arena Park, Rama. The vibrations were coming from your house!"

Loud gasps spread like wild fire around the camp.

"The drones?" Rama persisted.

With a deep breath, Michael revealed the dark secret he had been carrying. "The drones revealed Kriaka in deep meditation in front of the White Stone in your secret garden."

The men moaned. Rama leaned back and cracked the

tension in his neck.

Michael grabbed the chance to let it all off his chest. "When the Dragons stole the White Stone, my father began running tests on it and discovered that it was the key he needed to beam to the other planets. But each attempt to use it failed. He couldn't understand why. Pierre came that stormy night, last week. I'll never forget his dark, cloaked figure. The wind howled through the castle, and father was at his wits' end. Pierre said that Kriaka was the only one to activate the powers of the GIFT."

Rama towered, his hands behind his head, his eyes flashing red streaks from the fire. "Man, that's how he faked her kidnapping!"

Tears bubbled, and Michael gave vent. "I hated my father so much that night that I wished him dead. I only wish he was not my father." He sank to the ground and stared at the fire.

※ ※ ※ ※ ※ ※

CHAPTER SEVEN

Earthlings and Utopian Aliens

JALI'S HEART RACED. HE knew he had to act fast. *I must initialize one more Zookian Glass transmission with Reena.*

The petrified troops around him motivated him further. What other hope is there? Kriaka Adi is depressed over Doctor Herby, and now that the GIFT is out of the borders she may never recharge enough to open the secret Gateway and activate the Portal.

I may never get back home. And Grandma, what will happen to Grandma? I may never be able to protect Reena and any Zookian.

I shall be remembered as the one responsible for the collapse of peace and of time itself. Why did I sneak on to Zooble? Reena, the Commander ZW1, and the Magnificent ZW7 warriors would already be here, instead of powerless me!

His heart pounded as he observed the faces of the troops around the campfire. Their helplessness weighed heavy on his little shoulders. A decision had to be made. Immediately. There was no time to lose.

Prince Jali pushed his chest out and stepped away from Tuttles. "I am ready to contact Zooble."

Two hundred pairs of eyes zoomed in on him. His tiny heart skipped a beat, and his palms sweated. Clasping the Thermo Regulator Amulet, he stabilized his body temperature and prepared to focus. It would be the first time that someone other than Siya, Shiana, Meosic, or Brelize would witness him interacting with the Zookians.

Siya tugged at his hand. "But Prince, you have only one attempt before you beam up to Zooble."

"Yes, I must use my last message to help the beings on your planet."

A murmur around the campfire revealed the mounting tension, and Rama suggested the core team retreat to the leaders' tent. Majestic One, Junior, Siya, and Michael accompanied him and Jali inside. Brelize skipped in, and Tuttles floated above.

Jali's heart beat fast.

He closed his eyes as he stood astride in the middle of the tent. His Third Eye fluttered. With a deep breath, the young prince focused his energy between his eyebrows and felt the familiar warmth spread through his spine. It traveled up the back of his neck and lodged between his eyes. His Third Eye opened wide. A swirl of blue lights wrapped him and puffed out the tent.

"Reena!"

The team gasped, and the troops outside hushed.

The Control Chamber emerged with Reena and Commander ZW1.

"Greetings, Rama Adi, Michael, Majestic One, Junior, Siya, Brelize, and good to see you, Tuttles." Reena smiled at Jali.

Commander ZW1's solemn tone apprised them of the dire situation. "Greetings, Earth beings. Greetings, Prince Jali. You are correct. The GIFT is no longer in the confines of South Africa. Michael, we need you to uncover the last coordinates of the GIFT, together with its material composition. Be notified, our Zooble team can track the GIFT if it is in transport. The Impostor's Force Two occludes a scan of your planet's core. We can track the GIFT only if it remains above ground.

"Prince Jali, the Portal will be primed to open in fifty-six Earth hours. We have one chance to make the exchange; you for Princess Reena and our Magnificent ZW7 warriors and I."

Commander ZW1 continued. "Rama Adi, an SOS from planet Earth activated our Peace-Keeping Magnificent ZW7 mission to restore what has been changed in your world. In plain words, we need to retrieve the stolen GIFT and return it to Kriaka Adi, the Leader of the First Ones, before your planet completes forty-two nocturnal rotations. If not, your planet will perish."

The transmission was drawing to an end, and Jali longed for a vital report. "How is Grandma, Reena?"

Her face saddened. "I'm afraid Grandma is weak. She needs for you to be safe on Zooble. Rest assured, we are focused on returning you to us, Jee." And the blue light faded.

Jali felt every ounce of energy drain from him and he staggered. Rama rushed to his aid, setting him to rest near Tuttles.

Grandma needs me back on Zooble.

For the first time since the tragic day on Zooka, fourteen Z-years ago, Jali remembered her words. "You are the first male offspring of our royal lineage, little one." She had cradled him after news of his parents' fatal attack surfaced. Every utopian value essential to Zookian life was inculcated in him by his dearest Grandma.

The entire planet Zooka, planet Earth, the Cosmos, and his Grandma were at stake. He realized the urgency of his reunion with her, and he also understood that he was the only link between the pure Earth beings and Zooble. Somehow both missions were intertwined, and even though his young life form could not fully comprehend how, he knew he had to act.

"Michael, we must retrieve the last known coordinates of the GIFT."

The young man's eyes sparkled, and he pointed to the devices he and Siya had removed from Spioenkop. "We brought the main AIC systems, and we may be able to track the coordinates."

Without hesitation, Michael and Siya began assembling the devices in the corner of the tent, while the rest of team watched with bated breaths.

They turned on the devices, and a soft buzz rippled. But the devices quieted. "Oh no." Michael groaned. "We are out of the lab, so we need father's biometrics!"

"We can try a password to override the system," Siya suggested.

Michael agreed and for half an hour they tried numerous permutations of possible words, but each attempt failed.

Rama leaned and whispered, "Jenni?"

"Yes, of course, Mother's nickname." Michael appeared hopeful, and entered the password.

A sinister laughter ripped through the tent, and a song ensued.

"Try as ya might, ya have one more night before I extinguish your light. I'm coming to get ya!"

Jali felt his heart stop.

"Darn, we have to find the password fast before they track us down," Michael said.

Multitudes of iterations and permutations failed. They continued, in vain, until Jali had an idea. "What about Impostor."

Siya nodded and his fingers beat out the word. They held their breaths. The screen cleared, and they were in.

"Hurray." The group cheered.

"Now to find the coordinates and the composition of the GIFT," Siya said. And with Michael at his side, they pounded on the keys.

❋ ❋ ❋ ❋ ❋ ❋

It was well past midnight when Rama checked on the team. There was no progress, and from way he tugged at his cap Jali could feel his disappointment.

He shrugged helplessly, and accompanied Majestic One and Rama out of the tent into the cool summer night.

"Man, I hope the guys break the code. Without the exact location, we're finished." Rama placed his hands on his head and looked toward the parking lot. "The buses still not here?"

"Ay, no." Majestic One's voice sounded apologetic.

Rama kicked the sand. "Well, at least we—"

"Rama!" A young warrior shouted, as he ran from the lookout point. "Lights. Someone's coming."

"Stand guard." Majestic One commanded the troops to prepare for an attack.

In the distance a stream of lights zigzagged, sending Jali's heart into palpitations. What if Force Two tracked the AIC? He hoisted himself onto Tuttles, and they flew through the night sky, their heads haloed with fireflies. The campsite shrank into the distance as they neared the snake of lights, in the darkened valley.

"Buses." Jali's ears perked, and his super-hearing tuned in.

"Heck, I don't know which way to vaai; it's so dark. Are we on the right track? I'm vaaing back," said a voice from the lead bus.

Tuttles hovered closer to the driver's open window, and Jali attempted to solve the man's conundrum. "You are on the right road, Earth being."

"Ayo!" The driver lunged the bus to a stop, with the trailing buses screeching to a halt.

"Who's there?"

Jali had no choice but to reveal himself.

"Ayo!" The driver and terrified passengers screamed.

Their screams grew louder when they saw Tuttles.

"No need to be afraid, Earth beings," Tuttles said.

The screams persisted, louder. "Ayo!"

"Ayo," Tuttles repeated, in an effort to ally with

them.

But their deafening screams battered him instead.

From the last bus, a warrior ran forward. "Prince. Prince Jali? Wungani? How are you?"

"Lungila. I am well." Jali replied, and raised his thumb.

"Spot on." The warrior mimicked the gesture, reassuring the hysterical warriors. "This is the Prince that Shiana spread the word about."

His explanation appeared to appease the troops, who exited the bus and bowed to their superheroes.

"Follow us, we shall guide you through the mountain pass," Jali said. And he and Tuttles escorted the buses along the final dark stretch to the campsite.

"The buses are here!" Shouts from the campsite were heard.

Hollers of delight welcomed the long-awaited travelers, who broke into a dance inside the buses. Unable to resist, Jali and Tuttles alighted atop the lead bus and joined in the dance, as the joyful busloads came to a halt in the parking lot.

Rama, flinging his cap in the air, ran to them. "We needed this. Now it's all up to Siya, Michael and Kriaka to do their bits."

The tribal warriors gathered at the campfire where the newly-arrived First Ones wolfed down sandwiches eagerly distributed by the camp chef.

Outside the main tent, Rama and Majestic One poured over the ancient mountain map, avidly plotting the best trails to reach the cliff face of the Amphitheatre and Sentinel—on the escarpment from where the three majestic rivers of South Africa once arose.

The campsite quieted as the warriors fell asleep. But inside the leaders' tent, the race against time continued; Michael scribbled in frenzy and Siya worked tirelessly on the AIC, with Jali, Brelize, and Tuttles watching in silence.

Eventually Jali's eyelids closed and he nodded off.

✳ ✳ ✳ ✳ ✳ ✳

CHAPTER EIGHT

The Secret

Fourth morning

JALI LEANED ON TUTTLES outside the leaders' tent, and taking in a deep breath he basked in the brisk highland air. A scent of roses wafted to him, and he smiled. At the side of the tent, sunbirds pecked their yellow beaks into fairy bellflowers filled with nectar, teased by the imminent morning sun. Brelize's furry tail tickled his ears, and he burst into giggles as she ran down his arm and curled her paw around his finger.

He missed Brela, and most of all he missed Grandma and Reena. Today would be a momentous one, bringing him and Tuttles closer to returning home.

His pointed ears perked and tuned in to the stirring of troops in the campsite and a shuffle within the tent. He entered to find Rama standing over Michael and Siya, who were curled and snoring like thunder, on the ground.

"Prince Jali?" Rama's voice had an expectant tone.

Michael and Siya awoke, and leapt to attention.

"Well, guys?" Rama could not have twisted his cap more if he wished.

"Yes, we did it, we know the precise location where the GIFT last was!" Michael's high-pitched voice replied.

Siya chimed in. "We also have the composition of the White Stone."

The broad smile shed years off Rama's face. He patted Michael's back and grabbed Siya, and swung him in the air. In a flash, he straightened his cap, and turned to Jali.

Sensing his anxiety, Jali replied, "Rama Adi, Reena would have received the news the instant Michael and Siya discovered it. I am sure our Magnificent ZW7 are tracking the GIFT."

"Man! Okay, one down, two to go." He looked to entrance and his face glowed with happiness.

In the doorway, Kriaka stood tall, the curls of her long black hair and the silhouette of her slender figure shimmering against the fiery splattering of dawn. She wore a hint of a smile on her heart-shaped face.

"We're gonna find the GIFT, Kri." Rama kissed her forehead, and rubbed his hands vigorously. "Okay, we've a hard mountain trek ahead of us. Time to get ready!"

❅ ❅ ❅ ❅ ❅ ❅

The early morning sun cast her protective net of rays over the campsite as the four hundred nourished troops dismantled the tents.

Standing on what had served as the breakfast table, Rama and Magnificent One discussed the finer details of the treks, while the troops donned their trekking gears and assembled in front of them to receive instructions for the routes.

Tuttles and Jali coasted in the sunny clear sky, and hovered over the gathering.

Junior let out a shrill, "Yebo." And the roars rippled through the pack. The warriors stretched their arms above their heads, stooped low, bent their knees, and danced the warrior dance.

Eager to join the frolicking, Jali and Tuttles landed on a rock and danced. Meosic leaped onto the adjacent rock, stretched her sandy-colored neck, and meowed.

Brelize skipped atop her, stood on her hind legs, and together the furry pair gyrated.

Across from them, Rama cheered and swayed in rhythm with Majestic One. Michael, who was quietly observing from the side of the troops, reached to Kriaka and drew her into the intoxicating trance-like dance.

"Yebo," the troops sang, churning their energies higher with each movement and each chant.

Jali pirouetted around Tuttles as waves of joy infused his body.

When the dancing quieted, the chanting softened to a deep hum, and the four hundred troops split into two groups, to lower the risk of annihilation from Pierre's threat of an attack, and to guard the major access paths to the Portal.

Majestic One, Junior, and Rama remained with the lead group comprising of Kriaka, Shiana, Siya, and Michael. Their plan was to hike fifteen kilometers through an old Sentinel trail to chain ladders leading to the escarpment plateau on Mont Aux Sources and toward the sheer cliffs of the Amphitheatre.

The second group would hike to the Gorge and establish base camps from there along the seven-kilometer route to the foot of the Thukela Falls, and at each of the five cascades from the waterfall.

Jali and Tuttles flew above the parting groups, past Rugged Glen eastward and over the undulating trials soon to be traversed by the Gorge troops.

Their new exploits held wonder for Jali.

Tuttles buzzed. "Before the Dark Period, this area known as Busingatha was inhabited by the local Africans from the KwaZulu-Natal province."

But today below them, there were no humans. A movement caught Jali's attention. "Look, the elands."

They flew lower and closer to a large herd of elands.

"Prince Jali, thank you for scaring the poachers. Our

wilderness can now return to its natural state. Thanks to you and Tuttles." The lead eland continued, "The word is out that the day after tomorrow is the day of transformation. As you see, Shiana's call for help has rallied creatures across the land to support Kriaka Adi's attempt to open the Gateway and the Portal."

Wherever Jali looked, creatures were on the move toward Mont Aux Sources: mongooses, squirrels, white rhinoceroses, lions, elephants, giraffes, mountain reedbucks, zebras, and many more. The ramble stretched through numerous valleys to the far eastern ascent to Mont Aux Sources.

Multitudes of species were gathering to support Kriaka. Eager to apprise her of the news, Jali suggested they return to the Sentinel lead group.

They retraced their flight path and came upon Rama fully decked with a backpack, guns in his hip holsters, and a long-range rifle around his shoulder, leading the troop westward on a wide gravel trail.

Jali descended and hiked beside Shiana and Kriaka. Tuttles soared and disappeared behind them.

"Lord Tuttles." The voices of the troops echoed through the trail.

"Hayibo," Tuttles' voice boomed.

"Hayibo!" the troops roared.

Jali smiled with amusement, and he too wanted to

add to the exuberant mood. "Kriaka Adi, hundreds of creatures are on their way to Mont Aux Sources to support you."

She smiled but hiked in silence.

Deep in thought, Jali pondered on the yet to be answered question, and he hesitated for a brief moment before posing it.

"Shiana, at the Zookian celebration party, my Grandma received an SOS from your planet. When Zooble reached Earth's atmosphere, the Magnificent ZW7 team traced the location close to your home."

Shiana's large eyes merged with the brilliant blue sky; her golden hair glowed like a halo.

"Shiana, did you send the SOS?"

Kriaka halted and stared at her sister, with a look of curiosity.

"Shiana, did you summon us?" Jali asked.

She frowned. "N-no, Prince Jali, I d-didn't send the SOS."

Kriaka stroked the girl's cheek, and they continued, leaving Jali muddled. *If not Shiana, then who sent the SOS?* He sighed and shrugged off the nagging thought.

"Shiana, would you like to fly with Tuttles and me. There is someone I'd like you to meet?"

"Y-yippee!" She looked to Kriaka for approval, and on receiving a nod, she accompanied Jali toward Tuttles, who awaited them on the side of the trail.

His green eyes beamed, as he extended his right limb and opened his claw. She effortlessly stepped into the foot-holder and hoisted herself onto the shell.

"Hold on to my front shell, Shiana Adi."

Jali alighted behind her. "Here we go."

They slowly ascended, straight up.

"W-wow!"

On the extensive trail below them, the troops cheered, before the trio turned and flew over the short forest and eastward to the eland antelopes.

Shiana reached to Tuttles and stroked his neck. "Oh, look. So many beings are coming!" She spoke without a note of stammer.

Tuttles winked at her and Jali, with a knowing smile in his eyes.

"Yes, Shiana, we are indebted to you," Jali said.

They hovered and landed near the familiar herd of elands.

The leader of the elands nodded. "Shiana, we heard your call."

She smiled and blushed. "How lovely, I am delighted."

"Greetings, Shiana," the herd of elands said.

"Hello," she replied, redder than before.

"You can hear and talk to the creatures?" Jali asked.

She nodded and whispered, "You won't tell the others?"

"Not if you do not want me to.".

"Time to get back to Kriaka Adi," Tuttles announced.

They floated over narrow streams and rolling grasslands, to the two hundred troops meandering out of the forest and trekking into higher elevations.

Tuttles landed on a large boulder on the side of the rocky trail, where Jali updated Rama and the troops. "Shiana has amassed the creatures of the land. They are journeying to meet us at Mont Aux Sources."

The news rippled through the cheering troops. Meosic leapt onto Shiana and meowed, while Kriaka rewarded her sister with a kiss.

But Jali could not shake off his confusion. He bit his lip, and he skipped to Siya.

"Hayibo, Prince, what's the matter? Why you not happy?"

He pouted and sighed. "I thought Shiana sent the SOS, but she did not."

"Prince, it's not important who sent the SOS. I am happy that you came to help us."

"Perhaps you are right, Siya."

❇ ❇ ❇ ❇ ❇ ❇

CHAPTER NINE

Unforeseen Threat

SIYA, JALI, AND MICHAEL hiked together up the steep rocky mountain path. Behind them Rama and Kriaka helped Shiana over a mass of boulders, and Tuttles flew in plain sight.

Kriaka radiated a peaceful glow. Orange, red, and green mother-of-pearl butterflies settled on her long hair pulled in a tight knot behind her head, and on her sister's sun hat, purple four-footed butterflies flitted.

Suddenly, the excited shrieks of baboons at the top of the path startled them. Shiana toppled and slipped between the boulders. "Ouch." She tugged at her left ankle.

Rama hauled her out and placed her gently on the rock. Kriaka rolled up the girl's pants to examine her ankle and foot, and smiled.

"I'm okay, here let me see." Shiana grinned and

walked gingerly over the boulder.

On hearing the girl's fluent speech, Rama and Kriaka exchanged looks of confusion. They turned to Jali, eager for an explanation.

He smiled and nodded.

Rama laughed with delight and swooped Shiana on his shoulders, ignoring her plea to walk, but he quickly lowered her, as the group of chacma baboons, responsible for the loud shrieks, drew close.

In an instant, several of them swung down the path to Shiana; Rama jumped back with a startled look.

"They are harmless, Rama Adi. They have come to help Shiana," Jali said.

Each chacma volunteered to carry Shiana, until she pointed to the largest one at her side.

He raised his long arms above his head and shouldered forward, winking at Jali.

Still uncomfortable with the situation, Rama warily lowered Shiana onto the animal's back and walked at their side, shooting glances at the baboon.

Shiana rubbed the chacma's neck. "Thank you, Babloo!"

The troop resumed their hike under the intensifying heat of the Draco summer sun. Beads of sweat formed at the back of Jali's neck. He clutched the emerald Thermo Regulator Amulet dangling on his chest, and a cool wave surged through him, resetting his temperature. *Thank you, Wise One.*

Meanwhile, Michael, with the AIC in a backpack over his shoulders, joined Siya and Jali. The young man's face cupped with curiosity. "Tell me, Prince Jali, is your planet Zooka really peaceful?"

The image of Grandma, Reena, and Brela in the Royal Garden ignited a smile on Jali's face. "Yes."

"Who is the head of your planet?"

"Head? All the life forms have heads."

Michael and Siya laughed, and Tuttles buzzed above them.

"He means to say, who is the leader of our planet, Your Highness."

"Why did you not say so?"

"The quirks of our language, I suppose." Michael's fair face reddened.

"The leader is my grandma, Queen of Zooka."

"Grandma! She must be very old?"

"No. She is a hundred and twenty years of age."

"A hundred and twenty! That's very, very old! I don't think I've heard of anyone on our planet who rules at that age, let alone lives that long!"

"Every Zookian lives up to age one hundred and thirty, which is deemed elder, at which time they transform."

"Who takes over after your grandma?"

"My sister, Princess Reena, will be the next queen."

"Why not you?"

"Women have special super conscious visionary powers, suited for planetary leadership."

"And the men, what do the men do?"

"Our roles vary. Physical strength and strategic skills are used in warrior positions, and each of us assist in maintaining the purity of our environment."

"Do your people go to work?" Michael asked.

"Zookians *have* to work each day to grow food, to keep Zooka nourished, and to ensure the purity of the air, water, and land."

"Hayibo, your family must be laanis," Siya said.

"Laanis?"

"Ja, rich, with loads of money, and big houses, and fast cars, and planes." Michael explained.

Unable to understand the concept, Jali shrugged.

"You must have lots of money?" Michael asked.

"No, we do not have that. What is it?"

They chuckled. "That's what we use to exchange for food, clothing, and anything we want. Without it, people suffer."

Jali cocked his head and tried to understand the function of money. "Is it hard to find? Where does it grow?"

"Hayibo, Prince, I wish money would grow on trees! Aikona. We have to work very hard, doing all sorts of things to get it. Many people do very bad things to get it."

"Okay, so no money, but how do you buy things?" Michael persisted.

Jali shrugged again, feeling more baffled.

"Okay, so you don't buy food and other stuff?"

"Michael, each Zookian works together, keeping the planet clean and making sure all life forms are nourished with the fruit, nuts, and seeds that blossom each day. We share everything with everyone, and no one suffers."

"Hayibo, what about drought, Prince? You know, when there is no rain and no water?"

"The women use their superpowers to bring in the rain."

"Do the animals attack you, Prince?"

Jali laughed. "Attack us, Siya? Why should Tuttles, Elder Lion, or Brela attack us? We are all friends; we live together."

The boy nodded with apparent understanding, but Michael rolled his eyes and appeared skeptical.

"Doesn't it get very cold or very hot?"

"We have thermo regulation to stabilize our temperature. Mine is not completely developed, and I depend on the Zookians to reset it for now."

"Is that why you got sick here, Prince?" Siya asked.

He nodded and swiveled his Thermo Regulator Amulet.

"Wise One gave me this special amulet to control my temperature on your planet."

Jali's ears perked, and his Third Eye fluttered. Heeding his call, Tuttles swooped up and back down with a report. "Your Highness, an attack is underway!"

Behind them Majestic One commanded the troops. "Take cover!"

While the lead group scattered, Jali and Tuttles flew under the cover of invisibility. Past the rolling grasslands, puffs of smoke spiraled, and sporadic gunfire shattered the peaceful lowlands.

To the southeast tribal warriors lay trapped, ambushed by an armed flying craft, hovering over the valley. Its noise hurt Jali's ears.

His Third Eye fluttered. "What can we do, Tuttles?"

"Your Highness, we are no match for the helicopter and their soldiers. Your superpowers must be reserved for Mont Aux Sources and transportation to Zooble. If your capacity is below range, we cannot beam out of this planet!"

Jali moaned and watched in horror as the tribal warriors reeled against the gunfire and fled into the short forest. The helicopter landed and a bulky soldier jumped out, ran into the bushes, and emerged with a hooded captive, and the helicopter rose again.

"They have a prisoner!" Jali shouted. "We must alert Rama."

He clung on to Tuttles, as they zipped back to the lead group. On news of the carnage, Magnificent One and Rama catalyzed the troops to prepare for an impending attack.

Under the cover of rocks and shrubs, two hundred pairs of eyes fixated on the clear blue sky. Behind them, and still invisible, Jali and Tuttles watched in anticipation.

A thunderous boom resonated through the mountain trail, clouding the sunrays. Out of the gloom the helicopter emerged. Dangling from its side door, a gagged prisoner struggled helplessly.

"Wise One!" Jali's heart pounded.

"Hold your fire!" Rama commanded, while Majestic One quelled the troops.

A solider drew Wise One into the helicopter before it landed a short distance from them. Within a gust of sand and leaves, the force of which molded Jali against Tuttles, a towering man alighted. His body armor glittered, and a tyrannical grin splashed on his gaunt face. Two equally hulking armed soldiers followed on either side of him. The trio stopped a few meters from Rama, Magnificent One, and Michael, at the front line. An even stronger whirl of wind followed, as the helicopter rose and hovered above them.

"Magnificent One, we've defeated your warriors *and* we've a priceless gem with us." He pointed a long, gray cylindrical weapon at the helicopter, where Wise One was bound.

Raising his weapon in the air, he chuckled. "Michael, we are here for the AIC. Surrender it, or else we *will* eliminate Wise One."

The blond young man turned to Kriaka. She looked at Rama and Magnificent One, and each of them appeared to exchange silent messages.

With no response forthcoming, the leader continued. "We want the AIC only. We don't care about your foolish mission to Mont Aux Sources."

In the silence that followed, the leader insisted. "Hand over the AIC devices or Wise One dies in front of you, and we slowly massacre the rest of you."

Kriaka prodded Michael, but he shuffled and remained at her side.

"Michael, the Brown Witch is right: Wise One is important to you. We know. Now hand over the AIC or else." His soldiers took aim toward the troops, and in the helicopter, the soldier threatened Wise One's head.

Encouraged by the two hundred warriors, Rama, Kriaka, Magnificent One, and Junior, Michael unhooked the bag from his shoulders and laid it at the leader's feet.

The man grinned, and twisted his upper lip into a sneer. Steadying his weapon on his hip, he took aim at Michael. "You always were a chicken, hiding behind your daddy. We don't need him anymore, and we definitely don't need you. We rule his palaces and own his possessions. Yes, that's right, my boy, he's nowhere to be found! Dead, we reckon! I can now auction off the AIC to the highest international bidder."

He paced around Michael, and poked him in the stomach. "You picked the wrong side, my little man. You could've stuck around and joined us. You still can. Wanna watch us dominate the world?" He stretched his neck back and laughed.

Jali's Third Eye fluttered. "Tuttles, he intends to kill everyone."

Thankful for their cloak of invisibility, they rose, and without a breeze the flew to the helicopter. Jali peered through the open door, where the soldier and pilot appeared engrossed with the scene below. With caution, the little prince snuck in.

Wise One noticed as he tiptoed to the soldier at her side, and with his Third Eye projected a laser beam, paralyzing him.

While Jali had successfully freed Wise One, Tuttles had zipped to the scene below, disarmed the leader and his soldiers, and returned to helicopter.

The pilot startled at the sequences on the ground, turned to find Jali settling Wise One onto Tuttles, and he lunged at the young prince.

As they grappled, the craft flew out of control, luring the pilot back to the cockpit.

"Your Highness, get out! The helicopter is going to crash." Tuttles stretched his claw.

Realizing their imminent peril, Jali dragged the unconscious soldier to Tuttles, and reached to the pilot. "Come with me. Save yourself."

The man hesitated before pushing his way to the door.

Tuttles hovered closer and grasped the pilot before the helicopter lurched.

"Get out, Prince Jali!" Screams from below echoed in Jali's ears.

Alongside the plummeting helicopter Tuttles urged, "Your Highness, reach for my claw *now!*"

Jali's heart pounded as he rooted his arms and legs at the edges of the gaping door, and stretched one arm as far as he could, but the expansive gap between them deterred him.

He tried once more, when the gap widened, and his little body fell through the door.

The ground spun below him as he plummeted toward the screaming troops.

"Nooooooo…" Shiana screamed.

The ground swirled closer and closer, and her face became clearer and clearer, her voice louder and louder, when in a flash he jerked up into the air, to exuberant cheers from below.

Within moment Tuttles landed near the troops, as a massive explosion in the distance rocked the mountain pass, signaling the fatal crash.

Jali sighed deep and long. He could feel his energy return.

Tuttles rolled his eyes. "Ooka, yebo, Your Highness."

Jali raised his arms, clasped his head, and swayed. "Ooka, yebo!"

The troops cheered and began the tribal dance in celebration of Wise One, Prince Jali, and the flying emerald turtle superhero, Tuttles.

❉ ❉ ❉ ❉ ❉ ❉

CHAPTER TEN

The Gorge

OVERJOYED, JALI RUSHED INTO Wise One's outstretched arms and nestled in her warm embrace.

"Well done, little one. I see you found the one who flies. Your Grandma will be proud of you. I think you've earned more credits to your Level-5 graduation!" Her chest heaved as she chuckled, and her long white hair wrapped around him.

Kriaka joined them, adding to his delight. Even though she appeared relieved, a long shadow of sadness clung to her.

Wise One seemed to sense it too, and she reached out.

"My dear, First One, Kriaka Adi, I know of your loss. Fear not, for the good never die in vain."

Kriaka sighed and nodded slowly.

Wise One continued. "The positive force is still in

you. Since the Impostor invaded our world, our powers are easily trapped, usurped, and manipulated by him. But you can overcome it, my dear, by trusting your inner self. Look, Prince Jali has been sent to us for a special reason."

Kriaka smiled, and the celebratory troops surrounded them. A young warrior hoisted Jali onto his shoulders and extended the prince's arms to the sides. They danced through the throng, embraced by boisterous waves of cheers.

"Hayibo, Prince Jali." Triumphant chants echoed through the trails.

Jali bopped over the two hundred heads and winked at Tuttles hovering above. Together they had accomplished their third rescue on planet Earth, and now they could recommence their trek to Mont Aux Sources, to the mountain of streams.

❉ ❉ ❉ ❉ ❉ ❉

Wise One's presence further exhilarated the troops. Majestic One requisitioned four tribal warriors for a revered task, as Wise One lowered herself into a portable hammock, and they hoisted her new form of transport onto their shoulders.

"Ahead we go," they chanted.

Rama rushed alongside her. He removed his cap before bowing.

"Rama Adi, I know what you are thinking. What am

I doing here?" Wise One's chest heaved as she chuckled. Her white hair flowed over the hammock. "How can I miss all the fun? I've waited for this moment for many lifetimes! No need to fuss. I have the best travel arrangements, a bird's-eye view, and minimum energy expenditure."

Her adventurous spirit delighted Jali and the troops and even squeezed a chuckle out of Rama, who replaced his cap and smiled.

Their close encounter with the flying machine, troubled Jali. And even though the warriors had tied up the prisoners and confiscated their weapons, he felt uneasy. They had two more days before his departure, and he wished for it to be uneventful.

Around him, the troops resumed their trek toward the chain ladders that would lead to the top of Mont Aux Sources. Wise One bounced in her hammock, and behind her Shiana rode on Babloo with Kriaka hiking at her side.

Michael, with the AIC once more safely on his back, led the pack with Rama, Jali, Siya, and Majestic One.

"Michael, what did those blokes mean about taking over your father's possession?" Rama asked.

"My father was accumulating much power, working on many spells. I'm sure he was also dabbling in supernatural forces. He believed he could dominate this planet, by using the humans as test subjects to feed his plan of ruling the Galaxy."

"Hayibo." Siya tugged at his braids. "Galaxy. I've not even gone out of KwaZulu-Natal."

Rama grunted and shook his head. "This means he has amassed incredible power. I bet he has hidden resources and a fallback plan. A man in his position, man, I'm sure he knew he had sworn enemies out to take everything from him."

Rama's voice became barely audible. "I should have killed him twenty years ago."

Jali listened closely, and his super-hearing tuned in to the remorse in his tone.

"We came head to head that day after his marriage to my one and only love, your mother. But Jenni, she begged me not to stoop to his level. Now she's dead, and he's running amok. "

Rama raised his voice and his voice crackled. "Heck, do you think he's still alive?"

Jali caught his breath. He had not considered that option. What if he was alive?

Michael hesitated before replying. "Hard to tell. I thought he died many times, in many attacks on the castle. But each time that Pierre appeared, my father got better and became nastier than before."

Rama rested an arm on Jali's shoulder. "We must make haste to the Gateway, on time. I hope Kri comes through for us. Man, everything depends on her. All I can do is protect her and you, Prince Jali."

Jali turned, and on the steep trail behind them, Kriaka appeared deep in thought; her head was bent as she hiked.

Majestic One agreed with Rama, and left them to monitor the trail of troops.

The males continued their trek in silence, with the chants of the troops streaming to the front.

It was a song of hope:

"We shall overcome some day, hey, hey.
Our sun glows bright,
We dream of doves each night,
Our voices will soon have their say, hey, hey.
Their say, hey, hey."

Eager for a better view, Jali hoisted himself onto Tuttles. "Would you like to fly with us, Siya?"

"Yebo, Prince."

The boy's eyes widened, and he grabbed Jali's hand and propped himself atop the shell. He giggled and wrapped his arms around the prince's waist, and they rose.

"Hayibo, Prince, we can see the forest. And look at the klipspringer and bushbucks going to Mont Aux Sources!" He pointed at the yellowish-gray antelopes and brown bucks.

The boy's excitement brought a smile to Jali. He was pleased to evoke joy in his Earth friend, who had suffered so much.

"When will I be able to talk to the animals like you do, Prince?"

"I am unsure, Siya."

"I never thought I'd ever go anywhere out of our province. I thought I'd die early somewhere, like the other children. But now see, I can fly." But, the boy's laughter faded and he gripped Jali tighter.

"My mommy, she always told me, 'Siya, never lose hope, my son. Keep your dreams strong. Do all you can to help others, and you see, your dreams will find you.' I always dreamed of flying. Look, Mommy, Daddy—I am flying."

Jali's eyes welled, and he felt grateful as he remembered Rama, Kriaka, Michael, and Shiana who were left behind, without parents. Now the orphans had come together to help him to return to his family.

With his hands over Siya's, the young Zookian felt blessed to have met him. He wondered what would have happened if he had beamed elsewhere on this planet. *Why did I beam to that special spot?* And a thought occurred to him.

"Siya, did you send the SOS?"

"Hayibo. No, Prince. Wasn't me."

"Then who? Who would want us to come to Earth?"

"Dunno, Prince."

The river below caught Jali's attention.

"Look, Your Highness. That is called the Gorge," Tuttles buzzed.

Upstream, the river flowed out of a tortuous opening between two rocks and through the valley.

"Yebo," Siya said. "This is the Thukela Gorge where our troops will set up their base camp. But I heard people can climb up the wooden ladder on the side, and jump into the Gorge from the top."

"No need to climb, Siya; we can fly to the top," Tuttles remarked.

"Aikona, no fun that way. We climb the ladder. Come on, we can do it before the others get here. Tuttles, you wait for us at the top," Siya said.

Jali, wanting to experience as much as he could before his adventure on this planet ended, agreed.

"At your command, Your Highness." Tuttles landed on the embankment.

Jali followed Siya, boulder-hopping along the stream. On their left, a soaring cliff hid the rays of the afternoon sun, and on their right, as promised, a ladder hung from the face of a stretch of shorter cliffs.

His friend giggled. "Oh, what fun this is, Prince. What freedom. The Thukela Falls is just seven kilometers from here. Come, let's explore the Gorge." He pointed ahead.

They hopped over several boulders up the river until they could boulder-hop no longer, and Siya stepped into the water. Jali followed. He shivered from the icy chill, as they waded in farther, but the depth and current overpowered them.

"Okay, time to go up the rung ladder." Siya turned and guided Jali out and back onto the boulders to the river bank.

"You know Prince, at one time all the people from other countries would come here as tourists." Siya's voice sounded funny in between his teeth chattering.

"Tourists?"

"Yebo, visitors from other places. This nature reserve was crowded, and all those old buildings we passed at the entrance to the Royal National Park... yebo, it would be full of families and hikers. It used to be a happy place, so the story goes."

"Well, it is today. I *am* happy, and you look happy, Siya,"

The boy smiled, but his face quickly saddened.

"What is it?"

"I just wish I could find my brother. He'd love to meet you, Prince."

Jali's heart lurched, and he hugged his dear friend. "I am learning one important thing on this adventure."

"What's that, Prince?"

"Everything happens for a reason. I became stranded on your planet so I could make new friends. You, four hundred troops, and even more animals have become my rescuers."

"And we are helping you to graduate!" Siya hopped around Jali.

"Yes, my Third Eye powers are developing, and I am more self-confident today than I was before I left Zooka." He bit his lip and his voice softened. "I need to save my grandma now."

Siya pouted and looked down.

"Do not worry, Siya—Reena is confident, courageous, strong, and experienced. She has many Zookian superpowers. She is best suited to help your planet, not me. When I leave, she *will* rescue your beings."

"I'll miss you, Prince. Perhaps I can come visit you?" Siya looked up, and tears rolled down his cheeks.

"Yes!"

"Yebo."

They held hands and danced the tribal dance at the

foot of the ladder.

Siya looked to the top of cliff, from where Tuttles peered down at them. "Okay, let's climb to the top." He made way for the prince.

Jali placed one foot onto the first rung, grabbed the top rung with one hand, and switched legs as he reached for the next rung.

Behind, Siya held the ladder tight. "I got you, Prince. Go ahead."

Jali advanced to the next rung and the next. Below, his friend held the ladder.

'I shall be all right, Siya. It is your turn. Look." He scrambled up with lightning speed, and he grinned and waved to Siya still at the bottom.

"Hayibo!" Siya appeared surprised at his fast ascent.

"Hayibo!" Jali and Tuttles replied, before engaging in the tribal dance.

Siya climbed up fast and joined in the dance.

"Where did you learn to climb like a monkey?" Jali asked.

"I lived in the forest for a long while, and many times I had to race up the trees to save my black bum from the wild animals." He chuckled as he bent and smacked his bottom.

The boy raised his one palm in front of Jali. "Slap it," he said.

Jali grinned and slapped Siya's open palm.

"That's a high five," Siya said,

"High five. Yebo," Jali said.

"High five. Yebo," Tuttles echoed.

"High five. Yebo," Siya joined in, and they danced, in the forest plateau above the icy Thukela River.

"Come on, I'll show you the way." Siya skipped ahead, pushing through short bushes.

"I shall miss him, and everyone here," Jali said to Tuttles.

"Ooka, Your Highness. The pure Earth beings emit high levels of love."

Jali scrambled through hardy bushes, and up and down jagged rocks. Ahead of him, his friend appeared adept at crawling through tight spaces, especially the narrow crevice that Jali was stuck between. It was a steep and narrow ascent, with tiny metal foot pins wedged in the rocks. He pouted, unwilling to appear weak. And beside him Tuttles suggested they fly up instead.

Not wanting to appear unprincely, Jali persisted. If Siya could do it, so could he. He stretched one foot high up onto the foot holder and, pushing down on it, he clawed at a tangle of roots protruding through cracks in the stones and heaved himself up.

With a sigh of relief, he reached the top, to find Tuttles floating at the edge.

"You could have summited the easier way, Your Highness."

Jali grinned boyishly. He brushed his pants and hastened behind Siya, up and down rugged trails and out of the forest.

"Hayibo! See there's the Thukela Falls." Siya pointed ahead to the distance.

Past a series of boulders and beyond, from high off the mountain, the falls cascaded, crashing five times over caves in its path, but the friends were too far from it to experience its greatness.

"Come." Siya pointed to their left. "Let's get to the jump."

Jali followed until they stopped at a sheer drop to the bottom of the burgeoning Thukela River, making its way through the Gorge.

"Prince, everyone jumps here. We just jump too," Without warning, Siya jumped, letting out a joyful scream as he splashed in, and disappeared for a few moments, before popping out and shaking his head dry.

Jali turned to Tuttles, as Siya shouted from the bottom, "Your turn, Prince Jali!"

Tuttles buzzed and presented Jali with the facts about the depth, the cold temperature, and fall height, and he ended with the caveat, "Not recommended for first jumpers, Your High —"

But Jali jumped!

He shrieked with excitement as the water neared, and Siya beckoned joyfully to him.

Suddenly, his Third Eye fluttered and opened, as waves of iciness spun around him, fast.

He caught his breath.

His hands stiffened at his sides.

His body embalmed within layers of gossamer ice.

The little prince froze in time.

Motionless.

No breath.

No heartbeat.

Nothing.

❋ ❋ ❋ ❋ ❋ ❋

CHAPTER ELEVEN

Frozen in Time

Frozen!

I must be dead.

What is that?

In front, a figure floated. It disappeared around him and emerged at his right side.

What is it?

It circled him again.

And again, and stopped, facing him.

The fuzzy form crystalized and parted in two. One taller than the other.

Is that a face, two faces? Bodies? Angels?

Bright light bathed him.

No use trying to blink.

"Jaaaaaliiii, Jaaaaaliiii."

"Jaaaaaliiii, Jaaaaaliiii."

"Jaaaaaliiii," from the right form.

"Jaaaaaliii," from the left form.

Mama, Papa!

"My son."

"My son."

Papa!

"Ooka, Jali, my son. It is I, Papa."

"My son."

Mama!

"Ooka, Jali, my love. It is I, Mama."

"Do not be afraid, my love. You have fallen below your acceptable body temperature. Heed our words, little one. We know you love us, we know you miss us, we know you want to be with us. But it is not your time, little one."

"Now is not your time."

"Gather your energy. This despondent planet depends on your goodness, desperately.

"Grandma needs you to be alive.

"And ooka, your strong warrior sister needs you to be safe.

"You are the only male survivor of the Royal Family.

"You must protect yourself until your thirtieth birthday.

"You are never alone, my son. We see all what you do, and we are proud of you.

"Look inside, my love. You have the positive energy of Force One inside."

✳ ✳ ✳ ✳ ✳ ✳

CHAPTER TWELVE

Ubuntu Circle of Love

"WAKE UP, WAKE UP, Jali."

"Jaaaliiii, Jaaaliiii."

"Please don't die, Prince Jali."

Hands clutched his shoulders. *What is happening?*

Jali moved his arms and blinked. A spate of coughing wrenched his chest as he spat water, and coughed again.

Someone rolled him on his side.

Kriaka's enchanting face loomed close. She cradled him on her lap. "Hush little one, you're going to be okay." Her soft fingers caressed his forehead and she kissed his head.

His Third Eye fluttered, and he smiled. She kissed his head again and rocked him. Shiana sobbed and held his hand. Meosic and Brelize rubbed their furry backs on his legs, and behind them Siya hopped with his hands around his tearstained cheeks.

A roar echoed through the mountain pass.

But Jali shivered; his body trembled, and a deathly chill penetrated his bones. He could not stop shaking.

"Find the Amulet," a soft voice said. The crowd parted to reveal Wise One. "Where is the Amulet?"

Tuttles swooped down with the Amulet strung on his limb.

How did it break free from around me? It must have fallen when I jumped. But how?

Kriaka draped the Amulet over Jali, but he continued to shiver. Wise One rested her hands on Kriaka's shoulders and warmth spread from her through Jali. He closed his eyes. "We love you, little one," echoed in his head.

The little prince drifted to sleep.

✻ ✻ ✻ ✻ ✻ ✻

Jali's Third Eye fluttered, and he slowly raised his head. Fireflies haloed him, and outside the tent distant suns sparkled in the African night sky. Mini campfires blazed and wound downstream as far as he could see.

"Prince Jali is awake!" Shiana shouted, and hugged him. Meosic pushed past her, and together with Brelize they took turns to lick his face. Amid their embraces and showers of affection, the rhythm of his heart felt stable, and he no longer shivered. He could move.

He propped up and returned Tuttles's wink. Alongside, Siya's lips slanted down. Massive teardrops splattered on the boy's hand, and he hugged Jali tight and patted his back.

Kriaka, Wise One, Michael, Rama, and Majestic One gathered around them.

"What happened, Prince Jali?" Shiana asked.

"I am uncertain. I remember my mama and papa's voices. They said 'Jump.' I jumped, but I felt numb after that."

"Aikona! Hay Prince, you were stuck in the air. Hayibo, I've never seen anything like that," Siya said.

"Your Highness, you were frozen in a sheet of ice, in the air, for six Earth seconds. Then you plunged into the water. Siya and I failed to retrieve you. You were stuck in the river! I flew back to the troops and brought the men with me, but our combined strengths failed. Without known reason, after a few minutes, your body loosened, and we brought you out.

"You were heavier than lead!" Majestic One said.

"Then, in a snap, you were back to normal, only ice-cold," Rama said. "The rest you know."

They lingered around Jali in the tent, ablaze with fireflies.

Siya offered him water in his special grass cup, and Shiana laid a banana leaf with a yellow mango and macadamia nuts at his side on the hammock. Jali slurped, quenching his thirst.

"I saw my mama and papa."

Wise One looked at Kriaka.

Did they share a thought? I must be imagining things.

He bit into the mango and devoured the sweet pulp, in between gobbling his favorite African nuts—all the while his gaze intent on Wise One and Kriaka.

Wise One looked at the men. "The Impostor realizes the power within the prince."

Power, I have power.

"He is close." Her voice trembled. "We cannot leave the prince alone tonight. He is protected within our circle."

Circle?

"The Impostor weakened the circle when he took Kriaka Adi from us and tried to destroy her unique powers with Doctor Herby's passing. But now, we can rally together and heal the wounds. Come, we must strengthen the Ubuntu circle," she said.

The group encircled Jali.

"Close your eyes," Wise One whispered. "Breathe out, breathe in. Focus."

She held Kriaka's hand, and with the other, Rama's. Siya, Michael, Majestic One, and Shiana completed the circle.

The ground shuddered as strong, rhythmic motions rippled through Jali, and his Third Eye fluttered. Rose scent filled his nostrils.

I am safe and loved.

He smiled. He saw Grandma. She smiled.

"Jali, little one. You will be protected. Stay close to the Ubuntu circle. Stay close to the Ubuntu circle." And she vanished.

A tear from his Third Eye rolled down his nose.

Wise One opened her eyes and nodded at him. "Good. We must rest now. The Ubuntu circle team stays in this tent tonight. We are safe for now."

The faces of his Earth friends appeared serene, and they took turns to ruffle his hair. He received many kisses, before they prepared for the night.

"How did your Amulet get lost, Prince?"

"I am uncertain."

"How would anyone know about the Amulet's power?"

"I told Michael earlier today."

"Hayibo. I'm going to keep my eye on him."

"Will that hurt?

"What, Prince?"

"Keeping your eye on him?"

"Aikona." Siya laughed. "It's slang. It means that I'll be watching him closely."

Jali sighed and bit the corner of his lip.

"What's the matter, Prince?"

"On Zooka, we don't put our eye on any life form. Trustworthiness prevails throughout."

"Aikona, not here." The boy rounded his lips. "Not here. Here, only a few people speak the truth."

Jali shook his head in disbelief.

Siya whispered, "I think there's a spy in our camp, Prince."

"Siya is right," Wise One replied.

The boy shook his head, and his eyes widened.

"Yebo, I can hear you!" Wise One winked at him.

✳ ✳ ✳ ✳ ✳ ✳

CHAPTER THIRTEEN

The Power of One

fifth morning

A BRILLIANT YELLOW-SPECKLED butterfly with white streaked wings, flitted past Jali's ears and nose and tickled his neck. He squirmed and giggled.

"Mylothris rueppellii, your Highness," Tuttles affirmed, as the insect floated to Brelize, still asleep on the carapace.

Past them, the Thukela River gurgled over pebbles and stones in the valley of the Draco Mountain, and along its banks beneath a sprinkling of dawn the camp stirred. A hundred tent tops jutted near the Gorge and downward along the embankment, disappearing past a curve of the stream.

The Gorge troops huddled over low fires, ate their morning meals, and puffed rings of vapors into the frosty but brisk and welcoming air.

Neat stacks of tents, ready for the trek to the first cascade of the Thukela Falls, spotted the riverbanks.

Jali's unexpected incident yesterday afternoon had impelled Tuttles to whisk Rama, Majestic One, Michael, Wise One, Kriaka Adi, and Shiana, along with Meosic and Brelize, to the Gorge. Junior remained behind to lead the main troops to the Sentinel trail. And while Jali recovered through the evening, the two hundred Gorge troops had arrived and established the first base camp.

An overwhelming emptiness spread in the pit of Jali's body. *I am going to miss this land called South Africa.*

As if sensing his sadness, Rama popped out of the tent and, tapping his shoulder, pointed south. "Prince Jali, the rest of the Gorge troops will trek that way for seven kilometers, to the foot of the Thukela Falls."

"Thukela. Yes, we saw the falls in the distance yesterday."

"Yeah, Prince Jali; it's also called Tugela in English. In Zulu it means sudden. Thukela."

"Rama Adi, I sense a special magic to Thukela Falls. What is it?"

"I don't know about the magic. Perhaps Kri can tell you that part of it. But what I know is that we are going to the highest falls on this planet."

Tuttles buzzed, confirming Rama's assertion.

Their chatter roused Brelize, still atop the shell, and

she stretched her little paws, sending the butterfly back into the air.

Rama continued. "Yeah, there used to be disagreement about the height of this and the Angel Falls in South America, even though the locals claimed ours to be the highest. But since the Dark Period, the Angel Falls dried up completely, and ours, even though drier, is the tallest."

They sat on a rock, to partake of the chef's breakfast of mango and macadamia nuts for Jali, and a thick sandwich for Rama.

"Yeah, the Amphitheatre, where we're going, housed the source of the three main rivers for our country. The Thukela, the Orange River and the Vaal River. Thukela had the most water and flowed through KwaZulu-Natal to the coast and into the Indian Ocean," Rama continued in between chomps of his meal. "Sadly, all the rivers but the one we see before us completely dried up. There's a lot of sad history here."

Siya brought a chunk of bread and sat on the gravel beside Jali. "Yebo, Prince, history teaches that South Africa was once filled with bush people and Africans, like me. See my unique hair? Yebo, one of a kind. Many tribes lived here. But then the land was invaded by people from faraway regions of the planet, in the northwest. They used fancy ships to sail the oceans, and they stole land from people along their way around Africa and all the way to the northeast, to where Rama's relatives are from."

"Why would they rob the indigenous beings of the land?" Jali asked, his lips sticky with mango juice.

Rama reached over and wiped dribbles from his jaw. "Prince Jali, unfortunately it is the way of the humans here on planet Earth. If they are stronger or more powerful, they manipulate others to give them anything they want."

"What about love and compassion?" He felt confused about the culture of the life forms on this planet.

"Hayibo, not much ubuntu anymore." Siya looked at Brelize nibbling nuts from his hand, and his face saddened.

Rama pulled the boy close. "Siya, in the past, there used to be more compassion, but that was before the machines and robots took over."

"Rama Adi, where did you come from?" Jali asked.

He chuckled. "Yeah, when invaders conquered the northeastern part of our planet—an area called Indus, later called India, below the great mountains of the Himalayas—they sent us brown-skinned Indians, like my forefathers, to work on the sugarcane plantations here.

"The tribes that already lived here, and we the immigrants, were enslaved. But you know, goodness prevails, even in people who do bad things. So after hundreds of years, people changed, and we got our freedom," Rama said.

The Gorge troops eating along the river this morning were of various skin colors and facial features, and Jali now understood their history, and their fervent motivation for unity, peace, and bliss.

"We are free on Zooka. Freedom is good. People can be ubuntu—loving and compassionate—when they are free."

Rama towered above the boys and kicked the sand. "You'd think that, Prince Jali. But sadly things worsened for people of any skin color, not only here but around the planet. People wanted more power, more possessions, so groups invented big machines and then smaller ones to accumulate something we invented called money, and to keep an eye on everything that people did. Bummer, the world returned to slavery; slavery of the mind."

"Is that how your air became poisoned?"

"Yeah, Prince Jali, everything changed. People became obsessed with invading the soil, the water, the air, everything, searching for ways to get the thing we call money. You know, the funny thing is we got used to breathing, drinking, and eating the poisons, and living in noise. We just accepted it all as a way of modern life." Rama clicked his tongue and crouched as he ran his fingers in the Thukela River.

Tuttles, already in the water, splashed his limbs and buzzed. "My analysis reveals that the brain size of the human species on your planet has shrunk compared to eight thousand years afore."

Michael, who had been quietly listening in on their discussions, chuckled. "Ja, that makes sense. That explains why we are low on love and compassion! But Prince Jali, how is it that on your planet things are much better?"

"My grandma says that an advanced life form is one that can love unconditionally, treat all equally, and live life compassionately."

"How can that happen, Prince? How can we become advanced and stop hurting each other?" Siya's large eyes reflected pain from within.

"On Zooka, we develop super consciousness as we grow. And at age sixty, every life form automatically attains the highest level of super consciousness. We revere them and our elders."

"Hayibo, that's why your grandma is the Queen."

"You are correct."

"Is this what you learn in school, Prince?" Siya's eyes widened.

"Yes, Siya. Our Guardians train us to focus on the positive powers up to age fourteen. Thereafter we learn to use our superpowers of thermo regulation, flight, invisibility, sharing of thoughts, mind reading, Third Eye powers, and—"

"Time to start the treeeek!" From downstream, Majestic One's command reverberated up the river.

The Gorge troops scattered to gather their backpacks and prepare for their hike to the base of the falls. Jali would remain with Wise One, Kriaka, and Shiana, while Tuttles transported the men back to the Sentinel trail.

Jali watched in awe as Majestic One and Rama alighted on Tuttle's carapace, and he floated low. The reptilian opened his left fore-claw to form a chair. Michael winked and perched himself snugly within the front seat. Siya gyrated a short dance before hopping into the right fore-claw, and off they went.

Jali burst into laughter.

"Yes, little one," Wise One said. "That's how we got here that fast!"

Tuttles returned to transport Wise One and Kriaka on his shell, and in his two clawed seats Shiana sat with Meosic, and Jali secured Brelize into his Earth-boy hood. And they rose.

Below them, hundreds of animals from a variety of species were on their way to the east of the falls, and several hundreds of humans were hiking the Gorge trail.

"Look, everyone is coming." Shiana waved.

Hundreds of hands waved back at them as they floated low, over the river and toward the Sentinel mountain.

Tuttles landed ahead of the main troops already on the Sentinel trail, to the famous steel chain ladders. Junior bowed to Jali, before rushing to help Wise One off Tuttles and into her hammock.

And the trek resumed, with the warriors hoisting Wise One. Beside her, Shiana continued on Babloo's back, closely followed by Kriaka, twenty-five hundred meters above sea level.

They settled into the route through the Sentinel pass toward the steep slopes of the escarpment.

"Tuttles, what do you see up there?" Shiana asked, with an expectant ring to her voice.

"Shiana Adi, the giraffes, lions, klipspringer antelopes, white rhinoceroses, many varieties of frogs, and more are proceeding to the south slopes of the Amphitheatre from every direction, thanks to you."

She smiled, appearing content with the news.

"And the African tribes are closing in from every direction too, Your Highness," Tuttles reported.

"What tribes?" Majestic One asked, his voice high-pitched.

Tuttles buzzed. "Venda, Sotho, Twsana, Pedi, Ndebele, Tsonga, Pondo, Swati, Bomvana, Mfengu,

Mpondo, Bhaca, Xesbie, Thimbu, Mpondomise—"

"Yebo!" Siya shouted.

"Wow!" Majestic One ran along the trail, his feathered headdress swaying behind, as he relayed the news to the troops. Cheers echoed through the pass, and the troops danced, their faces filled with joy.

Majestic One returned, with a beaming smile. "You know, Prince Jali, the tribes have been fighting for far too long. And for the first time, they come together. Now I think they realize the enemy is not the other tribe, but within each of us. And for us to be loving and peaceful we must grow strong within. This is what they've learned from you, Prince Jali."

Jali's eyes glistened. "From me?"

"You, Prince Jali. You loved your sister so much that you wanted to watch over her closely."

"Yes, you are right. That is why Tuttles and I snuck onto Zooble."

The Majestic One nodded. "Then you got left behind here on our planet, away from everyone you knew. You have shown us what courage is, and what true love is. You have brought out the very best in us, Prince Jali. We thank you for that." He bowed deeply.

Jali's eyes welled as he turned and waved to the troops downstream, and they waved back amid cheers.

"Today, people and animals around South Africa are

gathering here to protect you, and in turn to strengthen their own inner confidence and peace of mind, so they can be free of the hold of the Impostors over their minds."

"Long live Prince Jali," Siya sang.

"Long live Prince Jali," the troops sang.

"Through my mother, Wise One, we learned about sister Kriaka Adi. For us humans, she is the one who will guide us through to a place of ubuntu, love, and compassion. So we gather to support her when she needs us most, so she can open the Gateway and the Portal for you to return to your people, and to bring in our rescuers."

He pointed down the trail. "You see all races here: Indian, African, Colored, Caucasian, and Asian of all faiths, religions, spirits, and beliefs, together as one. We will always be grateful to the little prince who was left behind, and who now leaves behind a better planet Earth." Majestic One bowed and joined Rama in the front of the procession.

❋ ❋ ❋ ❋ ❋ ❋

CHAPTER FOURTEEN

The Amphitheatre

JALI HOISTED HIMSELF ONTO Tuttles, and they soared to relish the wonder. The momentous trek to the Thukela Falls had amassed an impressive crowd.

Tuttles buzzed. "People of all ages heard of the mission."

Below, throngs of people hiked. Many leaned on walking sticks, stronger ones carried elders and frail ones. A myriad of traditional clothing speckled the trails as seasoned hikers followed the Sentinel troops toward the auburn glow of the Amphitheatre.

The once-idle air filled with a steady traffic of birds parading avian families: larger bearded vultures, bald ibises, wattled cranes, and the daintier sugar birds, malachite sunbirds, and more. "Greetings, Prince Jali," the orange-breasted sunbirds chirped.

"Greetings," Jali replied, as he rode low on Tuttles.

In the magnificent splendor of the afternoon sunrays, the feeble, the old, mothers with young ones, and the pregnant gathered at the first base camp on the banks of the Thukela Gorge; beyond them thousands of hikers lined the seven-kilometer stretch to the Thukela Falls, joining the second base camp at the foot of the falls and the base camps at each of the preceding five cascades.

Tuttles and Jali flew back and hovered over the last Sentinel troops, hiking beyond the tree line between the soaring buttresses and the towering Sentinel Peak of over three thousand meters. Farther ahead, the troops passed cutbacks and cliffs, as the pair flew ahead of them.

The duo arrived at the first pair of steel chain ladders, already spotted with warriors. At the foot of the ladders, a long line of troops, together with Wise One and Shiana, waited.

Jali waved before they flew higher, to the second set of chain ladders, clanging heavy with troops. He caught his breath and reached out as they rose through a swirl of white clouds. The mist tingled his fingers and face, and just as quickly they were at the final pair of ladders.

At the top, leading the troops, Rama emerged from the uppermost rung, followed by Kriaka on the adjacent ladder. They had reached the summit. On the ladder below, Siya mounted, gripping a steel wheel on the side of the upper rung and heaving himself to the next rung, until he too joined Rama.

Michael was halfway to the top on the parallel ladder.

Jali and Tuttles burst into laughter at the scene on the ladder beside Michael.

Clawing her way up was Meosic, and clinging onto her back, offering instructions was Brelize.

At the top edge, the sand cat sunk her sharp claws into the grass, and Brelize hopped off, bowing to the applause of troops around her.

Meosic rolled around, showing off her white belly before stretching tall on her hind legs and twirling her tail as she swayed.

Bidding the successful climbers farewell, Jali and Tuttles returned to the first set of ladders where Majestic One and Junior supervised the last troops. The pair landed, and the men hoisted Shiana in front of Jali, and Wise One behind him.

The females, together with Jali, soared with ease past the three sets of chain ladders. They flew higher and higher until Shiana gasped.

"Time for a little help, I think." Wise One extended her Tribal Cane past Jali to Shiana. "Hold on to her, my child."

It was Jali's turn to gasp when Wise One's thick white braids threaded through his arms, and wrapped around

Shiana, enclosing them snugly.

And they flew through the clouds to the western periphery of the great five-kilometer escarpment atop Mont Aux Sources.

Ahead of them Rama, Kriaka, and Michael were already leading the Sentinel troops across the sparse mountaintop toward the Amphitheatre where they planned to spend the night.

"What is that?" Jali pointed to a small dwelling becoming visible in the distance.

"Little one, that is our famous Thukela Hut, where people would sleep on this famous mountain."

In the darkening sky, the roof of the lonely brick hut, unlike the grass roof huts in the tribal villages, shone from metal.

As they landed beside the hut, a gentle breeze flowed across the mountain's edge. Eager to learn more, Jali helped Shiana through the entrance only to find the hut empty and uninteresting except for the wind hollering through the broken windows of the once avidly frequented traveler's hut.

Outside, the troops unfolded the tents and prepared for the night, high above the South African sea called the Indian Ocean.

Jali and Shiana joined the Ubuntu Circle team to explore the plateau. Around them scant tufts of grass peered through expanses of rocks and stones all the way to the north ridge, curving to form the Amphitheatre leading to the Eastern Buttress and the craggy peaks of the Devil's Tooth. The half-moon Amphitheatre, a sheer rock wall, embraced the Thukela Valley one thousand meters below, clearly visible, without a speck of clouds.

They continued their adventure, following a trickle of water eastward, against the outline of Sentinel Peak, to the highest point, Mont Aux Sources.

The stream broadened, flowing to the edge of the escarpment, plunging and crashing on five cascades until it struck the rocks about a thousand meters below.

Jali felt awestruck. What a magnificent planet this Earth was. As far as he could see, the Draco Mountain soared high, a grandiose display of its one hundred and eighty million years of sediments. Unidentified fossils, later known to be those of dinosaurs, had led the locals to believe that dragons roamed this marvelous range, and the Draco Mountain were named.

He leaned on Tuttles, and together the utopian friends reveled in their last evening, high on the magical mountain that would lead them home tomorrow.

Little campfires brightened the five-kilometer escarpment, now filled with two hundred troops and hundreds of people, and many more who were emerging from the Sentinel chain ladders. All races and all faiths shared water, bread, food, fruit, and lodgings. The news about Kriaka, Wise One, Shiana and Jali had spread far and wide.

Unable to resist, Jali perched on Tuttles, and they flew over the north edge and glided down along the Thukela Falls.

"Your Highness, before the Dark Period, after heavy rains, the falls would stream from several edges, not only the one we see now." Tuttles buzzed as they hovered at the first cascade. A group of Gorge troops waved from the low overhang of caves as the stream splashed over the rock.

"Look, many of the strongest hikers have also joined the troops." A cheer rose toward them, and Jali returned their waves.

The pair descended even lower to the second, third, fourth, and fifth cascades, where more troops and people waved and shouted good wishes. North of the final splash, heads spotted the stream as far as they could see.

The duo rose and circled to the Eastern Buttress to the southern cliffs, below which they found the animals gathered in caves and passes. A herd of mountain energetic goats clambered up the south ridge to join the throngs on the escarpment.

❄ ❄ ❄ ❄ ❄ ❄

CHAPTER FIFTEEN

Female Power

O N THE ESCARPMENT, SPIRALING away from the Thukela Hut, in the African night, thousands of heads bopped around tents and campfires.

Rama and Majestic One stood at the edge of Mont Aux Sources, at the midpoint of the Amphitheatre, with Kriaka, Wise One, Siya, Junior, and Michael, and at Shiana's side, Brelize sat atop Meosic. Above the Ubuntu Circle team, Jali and Tuttles hovered, haloed with fireflies.

With a megaphone to his mouth, Rama addressed the endless heads of hushed crowds, his voice carrying to the cascades below and beyond.

"Tomorrow, we bid farewell to Prince Jali and Tuttles, and welcome the Zookian Princess Reena, Commander ZW1, and the Magnificent ZW1 warriors to planet Earth."

Cheers resonated through the mountain.

Rama nodded and smiled. "We have suffered much these hundreds of years. So much inequality, disease, poverty, injustice, and hatred. We have lost many loved ones since the Dark Period. Even though we knew the Dark Force slaughtered those who dared oppose it, we persisted in the name of justice."

Applause echoed through the mountain pass.

"Now we can realize our hopes for a planet of peace, love, and compassion, because we have learned that the utopian place we dream of really does exist."

"Ay." Roars of agreement reverberated all around them.

Majestic One raised his assegai. "Our forefathers were heroes. We pay tribute to our Wise One who has led us through times of great pain, to guide us to seek inner peace, ubuntu, and planetary love."

Wise One lifted her Tribal Cane, and the crowds cheered. "We have waited long. The time is almost on us. But hear this, dear ones. We are not past the danger zone. For the biggest danger is yet to come." A deathly silence fell among the crowd.

"Let us be prepared, for one among us will rise against us tomorrow."

Gasps rippled through the mass, and as he gripped Tuttles, Jali's heart skipped a beat.

Wise One's long white hair flowed in the still

mountain air; the red San paintings on her arm and her Tribal Cane danced around her. "Let us be strong and bond. For only when we unite our love will we overcome the Dark Force and open the Portal for our rescuers."

The crowd cheered and waved.

A calm descended upon Jali as Kriaka stepped forward and joined Wise One. He descended and stood with the women.

Kriaka reached for his hand and raised it as the crowd cheered.

Her soft, melodious voice caressed the escarpment. "We have lost many loved ones, but the good ones never die in vain. We *will* carry their legacies for a planet of peace and people at peace with all beings, with humans, animals, earth, water, fire, air, and the very space we share."

The creatures and humans cheered.

"We have a little one here, a prince from a beautiful time, with a pure heart. Now we know for sure that the future is a peaceful one, but today even time is threatened. There is only one way that we can stop the end of time. We must harness all our purity, all our goodness, the very best in us. Your dedication to a utopian future will be tested tomorrow, which would be seven days from the time of Prince Jali's arrival on our planet. Only when we feel as one will we open the Gateway and the Portal. We must feel as one to let in our rescuers."

Kriaka and Wise One closed their eyes, their foreheads aglow with the halo of fireflies. The women extended their hands to their sides, took in deep breaths, and exhaled.

They hummed two musical notes. A pure high note—mmmmm—and a pure lower note—mmm. The hums spread through the hundreds of thousands of beings on the escarpment, at the cascades, in the Thukela Valley, and lining the path through the nature reserve. With their eyes shut, they hummed.

Rose scent filled Jali's nostrils, and he smiled, feeling like a light cloud.

His Third Eye fluttered.

The ground moved away from him.

And he floated.

Startled, he looked around, but no one saw, as the crowd continued to hum with their eyes closed.

He gently returned to the ground. Beside him, Tuttles winked.

But deep in the crowd, near the foot of the first waterfall cascade, a pair of eyes watched.

It saw.

✳ ✳ ✳ ✳ ✳ ✳

CHAPTER SIXTEEN

Wunamangaz

Sixth morning

AT THE TOP OF Mont Aux Sources, where the mightiest three rivers of South Africa once arose, on the cusp of the flowing Thukela River, the Ubuntu Circle team slept under the stars, surrounded by a vigilant troop of fifty ordained Ubuntu guards. Jali and Tuttles looked east.

It was well before dawn, when the Ubuntu Circle team arose. With sparkling eyes and purposeful actions they prepared for the momentous day.

At dawn, on the escarpment, thousands of campers stretched awake, they stowed away their beddings and shared water and food with each other and the goats. And in the valley below, the hundreds of thousands were waking.

Jali's face glowed from the rising sun.

In the clear crisp air, Tuttles's emerald carapace

glinted, the colors of the rainbow. "Today is our day, Your Highness."

"Ooka." Jali's heart pounded with excitement, and a broad smile filled his face. "Today we go home."

Wise One signaled to him. "Stay close to us, little one. Do not wander. You are being watched."

He frowned. From their vantage point, there appeared to be nothing peculiar in either the vicinity or in the activity in the crowds below.

Bothered by his lack of experience, he curled his lower lip. *I wish I was older; I would at my beckoning see beyond the surface.*

Soon! When he returned to Zooble, he would perfect his Level-4 skills and open his Third Eye at his will. Ooka, he would soon be on familiar ground. Overjoyed he joined Tuttles, floating above the men.

Junior had thirty of the strongest Ubuntu guards under his supervision, to protect the Ubuntu Circle team through the mountain, where they planned to discover the first entrance, the Gateway.

The plan was to relay messages from the Ubuntu Circle team, through the line of warriors, to the hundreds of thousands who had gathered over the two days. The relay team extended from the escarpment down to the first cascade and each cascade thereafter, lining the trail to the bottom of the falls, and stretching to the Gorge and farther.

The masses fixed their gazes as best they could on the Ubuntu Circle team, high up on the edge of the ancient mountain, where the action unfolded.

The time had arrived.

Led by Kriaka, Wise One leaned on her Tribal Cane and shuffled beside Rama, Behind them the rest of the Ubuntu Circle team and the guards followed, as Jali and Tuttles flew overhead,

To their surprise, Kriaka walked away from the Amphitheatre, southward.

Jali gasped. Tuttles appeared equally stunned. *Where are we going?*

The guards and troops formed a barrier against the throng of people as the Ubuntu Circle team passed, heading toward the hut.

Kriaka paused at the open doorway and entered, closely followed by Rama, Wise One, Tuttles and Jali. Outside, the troops encircled the dwelling, and the Ubuntu Circle team ventured in.

Sunlight flowed through the broken windows, making the hut seem infinitely larger than Jali recalled. Kriaka touched the left corner of the brick wall. She crouched and placed her palm on the ground. Rama joined her, and together they appeared to search for something, until Rama stopped and clutched at a small metal hook. It did not budge.

"Your physical strength is not what's needed." Wise One pulled a red thread from her tribal dress and handed it to Majestic One. He inserted it through the hook and, with little effort, yanked the hook. It creaked as he and Rama heaved open a wide wooden door and leaned it against the wall.

Jali gasped at the massive hole spanning most of the floor.

Without a word, Kriaka jumped in and vanished. Rama dashed to where she'd disappeared. "She's okay, I'll go next. He leapt in and reached up, his hands barely reaching the top, as Magnificent One lowered Shiana, Meosic, Siya, Jali, and Brelize to him.

A musty odor filled Jali's nostrils, and he coughed in the darkness. Fireflies haloed him as he scanned what appeared to be an ancient cave.

Magnificent One guided Wise One to Rama, and the troop proceeded with Michael and Siya trailing behind. They entered a series of tunnels and descended through shallow stony steps.

With Tuttles once more at his side, Jali breathed easier. His loyal fireflies lit the cold underground passageway, to reveal red sand paintings of ancient beings.

"These are ancient paintings of the San people." Wise

One's eyes danced with delight and her Tribal Cane swiveled.

Uttering gasps of wonder at the ageless insect fossils plastered on the rocks, the procession veered through a winding path of prehistoric tunnels. After ninety minutes, Wise One pointed past Rama. "There, there is the door to Gateway."

Rama's heavy breath and soft scratches on the surface ahead of them filtered to Jali's perked ears.

"I think I have it," Rama said.

Jali swallowed hard and tightened his grip on Tuttles.

Rama shoved his body against the camouflaged access. He pushed again. The wall gave way to a cave shimmering with slivers of light.

The guards remained in the tunnel with Junior, as the Ubuntu Circle team went through.

Jali caught his breath. High up in the wide stone grotto, light gleamed through a star-shaped array of cracks. Kriaka and Wise One stepped in. But within a few steps, the Tribal Cane would not proceed any farther, and Wise One motioned to Kriaka.

The young woman's mind was to be put to the test. Kriaka reached behind and beckoned for Jali. He descended off Tuttles, and joined her measured walk to the rock wall in front of them.

His breathing quickened.

She placed her right hand on the stony wall, and smiled.

He caught his breath. A blue sand painting glowed around the edge of her hand. *Where have I seen that?*

"It is time," she said.

Wise One turned and nodded to Majestic One, who repeated the message to Junior.

Jali's ear tuned in. "The time has come." The words rippled out, through the tunnels, out of the Thukela Hut, to the escarpment and down the Amphitheatre, to the first cascade and to the Gorge and farther.

"The time has come."

Kriaka closed her eyes.

Jali's heart raced. *This is it.*

He waited.

Kriaka flinched and she tottered. Rama rushed in, and grabbed her. He lowered her gently to the ground.

She stared at him with a helpless look in her eyes.

Jali blinked rapidly. *What is happening?*

Rama kissed the top of her head and whispered in her ear. She looked at Jali. He smiled reassuringly. Rama raised her, and she whispered to Wise One, who once more motioned to Majestic One and set in sequence the message.

Jali's ears perked.

"The time has come for all of us to be one. We are one or none. Let us be one."

Kriaka raised her arms to her side. Wise One mirrored her.

"Now," Kriaka whispered.

The word spread.

"Now."

The pure tones of the First Ones swelled.

Mmmmm-mmm.

The hum echoed through the cave, resonating throughout the tunnels and beyond.

Mmmmm-mmm.

Five minutes passed.

Jali's Third Eye fluttered, and his hand brushed against Tuttles' hard shell; in the background Meosic meowed and Brelize clung to Jali's ankle.

Wise One staggered, and Kriaka collapsed.

The Ubuntu Circle team rushed to the women.

"Wunamungaz, Wunamungaz, Wunamungaz," Kriaka said.

"Wunamungaz, Wunamungaz, Wunamungaz," Wise One repeated.

Jali's Third Eye fluttered as Tuttles shouted, "Get on board, Your Highness. Now! Rama Adi, get everyone out of the cave."

Rama carried Kriaka and ran, followed by the

Ubuntu Circle team.

In the tunnel, Junior and the Ubuntu guards stood, frozen.

"This way," Tuttles said.

They turned into a tunnel to the left and into a large opening, piling in as far as they could.

Thunderous footsteps resonated through the mountain and reached the tunnel like a tidal wave, rushing into the cave and ricocheting out. It paused at the opening.

It turned left.

Jali held his breath and clung to Tuttles.

They were trapped.

A colossal hooded figure bristling with weapons appeared before them. Its loud voice boomed. "Open the Gateway!"

No one answered.

"Open the Gateway, I said."

"I cannot," Kriaka whispered.

"Open the Gateway, now!"

"But I cannot."

In an instant, it grabbed her with one hand, hit her across the face with the other hand, and flung her to the ground. Rama hurled himself at the figure, only to be thrown against the tunnel wall. From the tight corner, Michael raised his blue gun, but the figure blustered it down, and with a flash of radiation hurtled him in the air, crashing him onto the rocks.

The figure grabbed Shiana; her blue eyes froze like a wintry pond.

"Open the Gateway! Do it, or I'll break her little neck!"

"Oh, please, please understand." Kriaka reached to her sister. "We need for all the beings gathered here today to hum in purity. If there is one among us who harbors impurity, we will not have enough energy to open the Gateway."

"What nonsense is this?"

"What she says is true," Wise One said. "You are blocking the energy. Wun-amun-gaz is you! You yourself are to blame!"

His eyes blazed like fireballs.

"You want energy?" He raised his weapon, and its beam pinned the Ubuntu Circle team against the cave. "You want energy? I have enough power in this baby to light up the entire continent!"

"Your energy is of no use to us." Wise One lowered her voice. "There comes a time when man-made gadgets are futile. You are not pure; you hate too much. You hate yourself too much. You break the Ubuntu Circle of love."

The figure cringed as if struck by lightning.

It uncurled, bit by bit. "You old lady, you dare

oppose me? I'll teach you to mess with me! I've taken over the Dragon's nest. This Gateway is my ticket to being the richest, most powerful one on Earth. I'll not be stopped by the likes of you!"

The figure shook Shiana and raised its weapon.

A shot rattled through the mountain pass.

Siya screamed as a body hurtled out of the cave and into the tunnel, disintegrating into puffs of smoke.

The spell was broken.

Shiana ran to Kriaka. "Akaaaaaaa!"

Rama's mouth was agape, his eyes painted with shock. In his hand, he held Michael's blue laser gun.

"You did good. You saved us!" Majestic One said.

Rama's eyes glazed, and he tightened his lips. "Come, we must try again, time is short."

✳ ✳ ✳ ✳ ✳ ✳

CHAPTER SEVENTEEN

The Gateway

THE UBUNTU CIRCLE TEAM reentered the Gateway cave and resumed their positions.

Kriaka, placed her hand on the wall, turned, and smiled at Jali. The sparkles from the fireflies danced on her face.

"It is time," she said.

Wise One turned and nodded; Majestic One relayed the words to Junior, and the message rippled outside.

"The time has come for all of us to be one. We are one or none. Let us be one."

Kriaka closed her eyes.

Jali's heart raced. *This is it.*

She extended her arms to her side, and Wise One followed.

"Now," Kriaka whispered.

Mmmmm-mmm.

The pure tones expanded through the cave, through the tunnels, and throughout the Draco Mountains.

Jali's Third Eye fluttered and opened wide.

The stone wall of the Gateway parted to reveal a deep cave, shimmering from the ripples of sapphire waves, swirling from one end of the grotto.

Where the Portal awaited.

Jali heaved a deep sigh.

Wise One smiled and encouraged him. "Enter the cave, little one."

Kriaka held his hand, and they entered. The earthling and Zookian halted in the center of the towering pyramid-shaped rock walls.

Tuttles and the Ubuntu Circle team followed.

This is it.

A shiver ran up his spine as he processed the cave's stone walls, splashed with San sketches of ancestral tribes and Third Eye people, and below his feet the blue symbol of the Lotus shimmered.

"You have fifteen more minutes," Wise One said.

"It is time, little prince." Kriaka smiled. "I hope to meet you someday in the future; perhaps you will recognize me." She hugged him.

The team took turns to bid him farewell.

Siya held him tight.

Rama carried him and kissed his forehead.

Michael bowed, and Majestic One and Junior saluted.

Shiana's eyes glistened. "I love you, Prince Jali."

He touched Wise One's feet, and she placed her palm on his chest. "Be well, little one."

Meosic and Brelize jumped on him for a final rub.

"Bye Lord Tuttles!"

Jali's time had come.

He edged toward the center of the Portal with his best friend at his side.

Reena will be waiting. Grandma will be waiting.

He waved to the Ubuntu Circle team.

He and Tuttles could go home.

They were ready.

His ears perked, his Third Eye fluttered, and Tuttles buzzed as a cold breeze chilled the cave.

"Oh man!" Rama said, and they all turned.

❄ ❄ ❄ ❄ ❄ ❄

CHAPTER EIGHTEEN

Dark Force Two

CHAN!

His huge form occluded the entrance, and his red eyes scanned the cave. With a glare he petrified Meosic, Brelize, and Tuttles.

Jali's heart flipped. He clung to the wall and skirted away from the shimmering azure Portal.

Rama bolted to the man, but a crack of Chan's red whip sent him reeling against the side of the cave, where he collapsed.

"You good-for-nothing. I'm not done with you!" Chan drew an ornate red sword close to Rama's heart.

In a flash, Majestic One raised his spear and Michael drew his laser gun. But quicker than lightning, Chan, with a puff of his breath, covered them in ice, freezing them where they stood.

Jali's ears perked; in the tunnels and outside and beyond nothing stirred.

Chan sneered at him, at the women, and at Siya. "Don't think you are going to stop me from the one thing I've been waiting for my entire life."

Siya leapt onto Chan, straddling him, and with his clenched fists lashed out at the man's cloaked chest.

But his thunderous laughter impeded the boy's attack, as Siya shielded his ears and slid to the ground, curling into a ball of agony.

"You little good-for-nothing. You want to harm me? Heh, heh. Like father like son. Your mother was a great help to my cause, you know? Yes, she was my first cloned human in space, and your meek little father could do nothing about it!

Siya's shrill, ear-piercing scream shut Jali's ears. The boy jumped and resumed his fit of punches, before Chan threw him up in the air, crashing his body into the wall, from which he sank unconscious.

"Son!" Chan shouted and paced around Michael trapped in a sheet of ice. "What have you done to yourself? Kindness will get you nowhere. Look where it got your mother?"

Jali's heart raced, his face fluctuating between hot and cold, as he waited for a moment of escape. If only he could get Reena, Commander ZW1, and Magnificent

ZW7 in.

He glanced at Wise One. She mouthed to him. "One minute, little one, to enter the Portal."

He sidled back to the Portal in slow motion.

Rama leaned onto the rocks and rose. "Why can't you fight like a man instead of hiding behind your Dragons and your weapons? That's why Jenni could never love you. You feed off others. You're not a man."

"What did you say?"

"You heard me. You're not a man!"

Chan wielded the fiery red sword from his cloak and without warning plunged it through Rama.

"Nooooooooooo!" Kriaka screamed. She draped herself over Rama's bloodied body. At her side Shiana wept.

Chan grinned and turned to Jali. "Now for you, little prince." A second red sword flashed in his hand as he raised it slowly.

Jali's Third Eye fluttered.

A blast rocked the cave, and Chan cringed. He doubled over clutching his chest. He looked up.

Wise One brandished her Tribal Cane high in the air.

Chan's body shuddered and lay motionless.

"Little one, go!" Wise One urged.

Jali's breath quickened, his Third Eye fluttered, and his ears perked as he turned.

A dark mist rose from Chan, permeating the cave, spreading a chill of icicles around Wise One.

"Heh, heh, heh," a familiar voice rumbled.

"Yes, I am the Dark Force Two, the Impostor that lives in each of you." The mist took the form of a long hand, its gnarled fingers and elongated curled nails pointed to Wise One. "You have stood in my way for far too long."

The hand twirled. Wise One clutched at her heart; her Tribal Cane fell, and she gasped for breath until she dropped.

Jali ran to her. "Save this planet, little one. Go!" She groaned and her head rolled.

Jali glared at the formless Dark Force Two lingering near him. "Who *are* you? Why do you hurt these beings? Don't you know how to love?" Tears bubbled from deep within him.

The shape shifted into a dark face stretching from halfway up the cave to the floor. Jali cringed as the Impostor growled, spewing icy vapors from its endless mouth.

"Love? What does love have to do with me?" The face tilted and roared.

Jali's nostrils flared, and his Third Eye fluttered, as he rose with determination. "I love Reena, I love Grandma, I love Brela, I love Tuttles, I love Rama, I love

Herby, I love—"

"*Stopppppppppp!*" The Impostor growled, and with its breath pinned Jali to the wall.

The fog gradually shifted into the shape of Pierre. The half-human covered his ears, winced, and slowly raised his head. Red sparks streaked from the sunken orbits of his bottomless eyes. "Yaaaaaa! I was once loved! I was adored!"

"You can be loved once again. Love is the strongest asset you possess. When you love you are blissful."

Fireflies haloed Jali. His Third Eye opened and projected a hologram of Zooka in the peak of summer where he played with his friends. Brela was feeding him cherries, and birds were chirping around his shoulders, and he was laughing with joy.

The Impostor stared at the scene. He fell to his knees, rocked his head, and smiled with apparent longing, mesmerized by the happiness.

Jali ventured closer. "You told me how good you felt when you were in love. We feel love all the time on Zooka, and within ourselves, because we live in peace."

The Impostor dragged itself to the crumpled body of Chan until it slowly merged as one. The body shuddered.

Chan rose to his knees a breath away from the hologram. His features softened, his eyes glistened. "Yesssss, love." He tilted his head, and as he clasped his hands together at his chest, he appeared lost in thought.

Jali whispered. "We *can* all live in harmony and experience love each day."

Chan's eyes glazed with love, and he reached to the hologram, and the air around him warmed.

Jali sighed with empathy.

Chan crawled into a ball, and his pitiful cries rent the cave, telling a tale of infinite sadness, deep loneliness, and sheer desperation, before his body shuddered and crumpled.

Overwhelmed with compassion, Jali reached to console him.

The body jerked into the air. An icy draft sucked the hologram into a vacuum. The shape shifted and blackened, as the Impostor rose once more.

It filled the cave with deathly foreboding.

"You think you can get rid of me. I am the Impostor, fallen from grace because of the Cosmic Laws of Force One. Exiled, I live in limbo, scouring the planets for lost ones too cowardly to access their own strength. The weaklings flock to me like beesss to honeyyy."

His curved fingernails pointed to Chan, who remained motionless on the floor. "I give them power. Just a game of chess, little one, just a game of chessss."

Jali edged toward the Portal.

"Now it's checkmate! I win. You lose, little Prince

Jali!

The Impostor glared at the Portal. "Queen Vraka and Princess Reena, I have your little Prince Jaaali. I'm going to make my meal out of him. Let it be known, the GIFT is mine, this planet is mine, your cozy Zooka will soon be mine. No one can ever stop me."

Fiery hot sparks shot out from the Impostor's nails and a searing pain shot through Jali's body. His vision blurred. He crashed against the cave. Out of breath, he dragged himself toward the Portal. Another blast ripped through the cave.

"Noooo!" He screamed, as the Portal shattered and the blue light pulsed and faded.

Carnage surrounded the little prince. To his left, Kriaka and Shiana wept over the bloodied Rama. Near them, Siya and Wise One lay unconscious. Majestic One, Meosic, Brelize, Michael, and Tuttles were imprisoned in ice on the spot. And Chan's body did not move.

Not a sound was heard.

Anywhere.

He was alone with the Impostor, Dark Force Two.

His little heart raced.

His green eyes opened wide.

His pointed ears perked.

He took in a quick breath, and his Third Eye fluttered. Warmth rushed up his back. He stood tall, and pushed his chest out, as his Third Eye opened. A beam of blue energy flashed out.

The Impostor laughed and brushed it aside. He clambered in spider crawls up the rocks.

Jali radiated a second beam to Tuttles, and releasing him in all his fury. Jali jumped onto his reptilian counterpart, and they flew in a cloak of invisibility.

The Impostor puffed frosty mists, missing the duo, trailing showers behind them.

"You amuse me." The Impostor chuckled. "I've not had this much fun for light years. Surely you remember, your Guardian 1 has not graduated you? Your infantile powers fail you, little Prince; you are no match for me! Take this!" He raised his hand, and evaporated their cloak of invisibility.

Tuttles darted in and out of sprays of ice blasts until the Impostor drew in his breath and sucked them to him. He ripped Jali off the carapace.

Tuttles clawed the Impostor's ears before being hurled against the cave and falling in a heap.

"*Tuttles*!"

"He's a Tuttlet now! Ha ha ha. I think I'll have him as a side dish of Tuttlets once I'm done with you!" The Impostor sneered. "Now let's *see* what secrets you have for me?"

He grabbed Jali by the neck and looked deep into his

eyes. Jali's Third Eye fluttered and opened wide.

Battle scenes flashed in front of him.

"Papa," he whispered.

The Impostor dropped him.

Jali fell hard and his heart skipped a beat. He wiped his bleeding mouth and stared at the towering Impostor hovering over him.

Out of the stillness...

Chan choked for breath.

The Impostor groaned. He clutched his chest and gasped for breath. He moaned and staggered to Chan. With one hand, he grabbed Chan's limp form. He raised the other hand to the ceiling, and they flew above.

"I let you go this time, Prince." The Impostor muttered. "Heh heh heh, like father like son!"

Goose bumps formed on Jali's perked ears.

The Impostor grinned, with a look of victory. "Oh, how I love flitting through time. I must say I enjoyed destroying your papa."

Jali gasped and curled into a tight ball.

"Yes, little Prince, I terminated your mama and papa, and I will have you too. Not today. But soon."

An emptiness settled deep in the pit of Jali's heart.

The Impostor laughed. "You've brought excitement in my life. I think I'll keep you alive for now. I have the GIFT. This planet is mine!"

Jali sobbed.

"Go crying back to Grandma; relish your time on your utopian Zooka. It will all be mine sooner than Vraka thinks. I *will* rule the Cosmos, once more." He winked at Kriaka. "And you, my Delight, my Delight, you *will* be my queen. My Delight."

Taking Chan with him, through the tiny crack high in the cave, the Impostor vanished

Vestiges of his sinister laughter resonated against the rocks, breaking the hold over the prisoners, and Meosic, Brelize, Michael, and Majestic One unfroze.

"What happened?" Siya winced as he regained consciousness.

They ran to the crumpled bodies of Rama and Wise One.

Jali remained petrified in the middle of the cave. Tuttles, his skin and shell fully regenerated, rushed to the prince.

"Tuttles, he killed Mama and Papa." Jali sobbed until a hum captured his attention.

A weak sapphire pulse emitted from the Portal.

✳ ✳ ✳ ✳ ✳ ✳

CHAPTER NINETEEN

Going Home

THE PORTAL PULSED OUT of rhythm, its blue light dimmed in and out. Jali's Third Eye scanned the cave. Wise One had regained consciousness and rested against Majestic One.

Jali rushed to Rama, who gasped for air, the red sword lodged deep in his side. Kriaka and Shiana held his hands.

"Tuttles, what is Rama's chance of surviving if we remove the sword?" Jali asked.

"One in two, Your Highness. Rama Adi's chance of dying if the sword is not removed is one hundred percent."

"We must remove the sword."

Kriaka rose and spoke in a confident voice. "I'll pull out the sword. We can now access the power of our people." She nodded to Majestic One, who relayed the message.

"Bring on the powers of our pure ones."

A hum echoed through the tunnel.

"Mmmmm-mmm." It filled the air and entered the cave.

Jali focused his Third Eye where the sword lay wedged.

In a clean swoop, Kriaka pulled the sword and fell back from its weight.

Jali's Third Eye opened. It beamed blue light over the wound, sealing it shut.

The Ubuntu Circle team cheered.

"Tuttles, what are his chances of survival?"

"Excellent, Your Highness."

Wise One leaned on her Tribal Cane and urged Jali to enter the Portal. "It's now or not at all, little one!"

He agreed and touched her feet.

She closed her eyes. "Bless you, little one."

He turned to the Ubuntu Circle team. "Pure beings, you will find the GIFT with Reena's assistance."

They bowed, and Jali and Tuttles approached the Portal.

Kriaka motioned to Majestic One, before extending her arms, and closing her eyes.

A familiar hum resonated in the cave. All gazes fixed on Jali and Tuttles.

Jali opened his Third Eye, focused his energy, and the countdown began.

10...9...8...7...6...5...4...3...2...1...0.

A swirl of radiant azure bathed him, and the Portal opened.

He squinted. *Ooka, it worked! I'm going home.*

Within the Portal, Reena, Commander ZW1, and the Magnificent ZW7 warriors became visible.

He smiled. But in an instant his ears perked.

Something is wrong.

Reena frowned. "Jali, listen carefully. The Portal was damaged by the Impostor and renders our Transporter ineffective."

Not again! Will I ever go home? His heart sank.

"We cannot enter the planet, Jee."

He gasped. This could not be happening.

"Hush, Jee. Listen. *You* can be extracted. The Portal will allow you through."

Thrilled with the possibility of connecting with Grandma, he smiled. "What about the GIFT, Reena?"

Reena addressed the Ubuntu Circle team. "We have tracked the GIFT to a western area of the country you call the United States, in a place named Los Angeles. Our Z-Locator uncovered a second Portal, farther north, scheduled for activation within fourteen Earth days. Kriaka Adi, if you regroup there with pure beings and open the Portal, we will enter your planet and recover the GIFT."

Kriaka nodded, and her eyes shone with hope.

"Come, Jee, you can now transport through to us," Reena said.

He felt relieved. The Earth beings could secure the second Portal and proceed to retrieve the GIFT with Reena's aid.

Jali once again bid farewell to each of the Ubuntu Circle team whom he had grown to love over his seven-day adventure on their planet.

Their eyes glistened, and tears streamed down Siya and Shiana's faces. Brelize waved from atop Meosic, and the sand cat purred.

Reena reached to him. "Come, little Jee."

He extended his hand to her and raised his right foot to the shimmering blue rings, with Tuttles floating beside him

He turned one last time to his Earth friends.

They waved and smiled.

"Yebo," Jali said.

"Yebo," Tuttles said.

"Yebo," the Earth friends said, and their eyes flowed with tears.

Jali's Third Eye fluttered, a tear rolled from it, and his little heart pounded.

He lowered his outstretched hand.

"Reena, my work on planet Earth is not complete. I cannot leave!"

✳ ✳ ✳ ✳ ✳ ✳

CHAPTER TWENTY

The Gift of Virtue

"JALI!" REENA'S THIRD EYE opened, and her voice crackled. "Come, little brother, we will enter planet Earth in fourteen days. You must join us. Grandma awaits."

He retracted his foot and stood still.

Commander ZW1 tried to reassure him. "Prince Jali, now is the one guaranteed chance of you returning to Zooble. If you do not enter the Portal, we are unsure of your survival."

"No Reena, no Commander ZW1! I promised the beings that you *will* join them today and rescue them, but the exchange remains impossible. As Prince of Zooka, I am obliged to remain and assist the Ubuntu Circle team to prepare the second Portal so you can take my place."

Commander ZW1 disagreed. "Prince Jali, you have

not graduated to Level-5, and with limited superpowers and without stable thermo regulation you could be in grave danger if you remain unprotected, and at the mercy of the Impostor."

"I *can* perfect my superpowers here on the planet, with Tuttles's help. Reena, please. I must remain and represent the Peace-Keeping Force. The Portal, Reena, help guide us to the second Portal."

"Time is short. The Portal is ready to close," Commander ZW1 said. "Prince Jali, remember you can use the Zookian Glass to reach us, but your thermo regulator is immature, and the Thermo Regulator Amulet is your only protection."

He agreed, but his mind sought a vital piece of information before their communication ended. "Reena, is it true? Did the Impostor kill Mama and Papa?"

She extended her hand to him. "Jali, you have stepped back in time. Everything you do will alter the future, but you must understand the importance of not altering what must not be changed. You need to focus on opening the second Portal so we can enter, and remember, dear brother, even though we can observe you, we cannot intervene."

She sighed and turned her palm up to him.

"Grandma and I and all of Zooka are proud of you, Prince Jali."

Reena, Commander ZW1, and the Magnificent ZW7 warriors saluted.

The Portal pulsed and closed.

The cave darkened.

Fireflies swarmed over him, brightening the grotto. Jali turned to the Ubuntu Circle team. Their faces registered shock.

Silence pervaded, until Siya and Shiana ran to him.

"Yebo," Siya said.

"Yebo," Shiana said.

"Yebo," Jali said.

"Yebo," Tuttles said.

They danced together with Meosic and Brelize in the cave, deep in the magical Mont Aux Sources, in the Draco Mountain range in the heart of South Africa.

A roar echoed in from outside. "Yebo."

Wise One's hair flowed around her. She smiled and opened her arms to Jali and embraced him. Her Tribal Cane pirouetted at their side.

"Queen Vraka is proud of you, my little one. You have the makings of a king."

Kriaka ruffled his hair, but she had a look of concern. "Prince Jali, I know you want to help us, and even though we cannot assure you of protection from the Impostor, we pledge to protect you with our lives."

Rama agreed. He raised Jali in the air. "Prince Jali,

you are a brave youngster. I misjudged your virtue when you first fell from the sky!"

Michael, his head low on his chest, shuffled nervously. "I am ashamed of my father. He succumbed to the powers of the Impostor and turned against his own family and all that is good. I don't profess to understand what just happened, or anything that he or the evil monster said about your parents, Prince Jali. But rest assured, I will do everything in my power to protect you here on our planet and to assist our Ubuntu Circle team to open the second Portal and recover the GIFT."

Jali smiled at the words of encouragement pouring forth from his Earth friends.

Majestic One bowed low. His large black eyes twinkled as he flashed a brilliant smile. "You have chosen to stay with us, instead of return to the safety of your people. I admire you, Prince Jali. You are my hero."

"Yebo!" the team sang.

A wave of applause echoed around Mont Aux Sources through the tunnels to them.

* * * * * *

CHAPTER TWENTY-ONE

Ooka

RHYTHMIC DRUMBEATS CASCADED OVER Jali inside the stony hole, and he smiled as Rama lifted him from the tunnel and up onto the sun-drenched floor of the Thukela Hut, on Mont Aux Sources.

Majestic One jumped out of the pit, hoisted Jali onto his shoulders, and strode to the ten thousand humans and animals dancing the tribal dance on the five-kilometer expanse of the escarpment.

The Ubuntu Circle team gathered around him, and the crowd cheered as Majestic One extended Jali's arms and bent low, swaying into the dance.

"Ooka! Prince Jali."

"Ooka! Lord Tuttles."

Jali smiled and waved.

He looked at Tuttles, who floated at his side, and they shared a thought!

"Hayibo!"

✳ ✳ ✳ ✳ ✳ ✳

Enꝺ Of Book iii:

Щ.ußamåñǧɑz

Taming The Impostor Saga
Adventure Time Travel Fantasy Series

Reaꝺ On

Ebooks, paperbacks and audiobooks:

Book i: Ꝺance of Fireflieş

Book ii: Ꝺïkónå

Book iii: Щ.ußamåñǧɑz

✳ ✳ ✳ ✳ ✳ ✳

JUST FOR YOU

I hope you enjoyed ꓲꓲꓲꞁꓯꓟꓯꓠꓖꓯꓜ Book iii in Taming The
Impostor Saga Fantasy Adventure.
I'd love for you to **Leave Your Review**.
***

If after you leave your review, you would like to **join my
VIP Team of First Readers** for upcoming books, go here:
DrVie.com/ARC-Team
***

Want To Know More About The African location?
Go to DrVie.com/Taming-The-Impostor-map
***

GIFT FOR YOU

Receive your **free short story:**
Prequel to Taming The Impostor Saga
and special deals on my books.
DrVie.com/VIPfreebooks

✳ ✳ ✳ ✳ ✳ ✳

CONNECT WITH ME

Say hello or let me know how I can be of help to you and loved ones.

DrVie.com (main site)
facebook.com/ScientistDoctorVie
twitter.com/DrVie
Youtube.com/DrVieSuperfoods
Instagram.com/Doctor.Vie

I thank you for your support which helps me mentor thousands of youth for free through my global Super-Conscious Humanity Youth Program

✻ ✻ ✻ ✻ ✻ ✻

ABOUT DR. SHERI VIE

My dear Reader,

Life sure is an adventure, even with family and friends.

For me, my youthful adventures really began solo when I left South Africa to study in the USA-certainly uncommon in those days, for a single Indian female.

Since then, I've been living in six countries, twenty plus cities...on my own. A real-life adventure; new places, a variety of people, numerous cultures, exotic foods, foreign languages and of course endless challenges.

What truly amazed me beyond the fascinating cities, towns and traditions, were the breathtaking natural environments as I hiked high up in the mountain trails around the globe, sometimes with a guide and most often on my own. The African ranges to the Himalayan peaks. Pristine air, sounds of nature, and the splendor of fauna and flora in their natural habitat resonated with me. Staring into the eyes of a young deer, strolling adjacent alongside a giraffe, and reveling in the dainty clasp of a humming bird on my finger.

When I'm not exploring mountains, I share stories of my adventures to tens of thousands of all ages, from tiny tots to the 100+, in poverty stricken villages to plush halls.

What a joy to witness their personal transformations. I love inspiring our fellow humans.

My rewards come from the excitement in their eyes, the smiles that fill their faces, and the abundant hugs after each session. My work is my personal journey, and I live a simple life, pouring any revenue back into my volunteer work around the globe.

Now, I share many of the adventurous stories through my writings tinged with fantasy. I'd love for you to explore my books and send me your thoughts and feedback. It's a small world bounding with adventure, and I would love to hear yours.

Do invite me to inspire and motivate your group and loved ones, anywhere in our world.

Lots of love, and hugs,

Always,

V.

* * * * * *

CHARACTERS ON UTOPIAN PLANET ZOOKA

Books i - iii

Brela (Jali's Zookian squirrel friend)

Commander ZW1 (Chief of the Peace-Keeping Force)

Elder Lion (Zookian)

Green Tortoise (Zookian)

Guardian 1 (Jali's Teacher)

Jali (Reen'as brother, Queen Vraka's grandson)

Jee (Reena's nick name for Jali)

Mama (Jali's & Reena's mother)

Magnificent ZW7 (Zookian special warriors)

Papa (Jali's & Reena's father)

Peace-Keeping Force (Cosmic Peace Keepers)

Prince Jali (Reena's brother)

Princess Reena (Jali's sister, Queen Vraka's granddaughter)

Protector 1 (Queen Vraka's Advisor)

Queen Vraka (Jali & Reena's Grandma, Queen of Zooka)

Reena (Jali's sister, Queen Vraka's granddaughter)

Tuttles (Jali's Zookian turtle friend)

❄ ❄ ❄ ❄ ❄ ❄

CHARACTERS ON APOCALYPTIC PLANET EARTH

Books i- iii

Big Boss (supervisor of African warriors)

Brelize (Jali's squirrel Earth friend)

Chan (Michael's father, Dragon leader)

Dragons (Chan's evil gang)

First Ones (pure beings)

Herby (doctor, Doctor Jekyll, Kriaka's fiance)

Ivan (Dragon)

Junior (son of Majestic One)

Kriaka Adi (leader of First Ones, Brown Witch)

Kri (Kriaka's pet name)

Meosic (Shiana's sand cat)

Majestic One (African tribal leader)

Michael (Chan's son)

Miss Amber (school teacher)

Pierre (supposed follower?)

Rama Adi (Mr. Hyde, Kriaka's brother, previous leader of First Ones)

Saks (Dragon)

Shiana (Ana, Kriaka's sister)

Siya (Shiana's friend)

Tribal Teacher (African teacher)

Vincent (Siya's brother)

Wise One (mystical African elder)

✳ ✳ ✳ ✳ ✳ ✳

WORLD ON UTOPIAN PLANET ZOOKA

Books i - iii

Control Chamber (in Zooble)

Cosmo 13

Cosmos

Field of Detection

Force-1 (positive energy)

Force-1 Shield

Galaxy Al86

Level-4 (Graduation level)

Level-5 (Graduation level)

Lotus Wand (Queen Vraka's ancient spear)

Magical Arrows of Power (Princess Reena's weapons)

Magnificent ZW7 (Zookian special warriors)

Peace-Keeping Force

P1 invisible shield

planet Zooka

Royal Bed

Royal Cave

Royal (Counsel) Chamber

Royal Garden

Royal Guardian

Royal Observation Chamber

Royal Zooble Chamber

Spear of V (Princess Reena's weapon)

Summit (hideout to watch Zooble Dome)

Sword of Khadga (Princess Reena's weapon)

Telepathy (communicate via thoughts)

Third Eye (super-conscious powers)
Transporter (to beam over/to cross over)
Utopia (perfect place)
Z-Clock
Z-days
Z-seconds
Zarp-speed
Zooble Dome (lift off deck for space ships)
Zooble intergalactic space explorer
Zooka (planet)
Zookian (life-form)
Zookian Glass (hologram communicator)
Zookian Locator (detect intergalactic places)
Zookian-months
Zookish (language on Zooka)

✻ ✻ ✻ ✻ ✻ ✻

WORLD ON APOCALYPTIC PLANET EARTH
Books i - iii

Africa (continent)

Arena Park (town in Chatsworth)

Basotho Land (country adjacent South Africa)

Cathedral Peak (mountain area)

Champagne Valley (mountain area)

Chatsworth (area in Kwa-Zulu Natal)

Draco (Dragon mountain)

Drakensberg (mountain range)

First Ones (Kriaka's pure team)

(dark) Force Two (negative force)

Giant's Castle (mountain area in Drakensberg)

Gateway (first opening to Portal)

GIFT (mysterious stone)

Jen (bakkie, Rama's truck)

KwaZulu-Natal (eastern province of South Africa)

laanis (rich ones)

Mercedes (fancy car)

Milky Way

Monks Cowl (mountain range)

Mooi River (town)

Mont Aux Sources (mountain at the source)

planet Earth

Portal

rainbow nation (united in diversity)

South Africa (country on continent of Africa)

Unit 1 (township area in Chatsworth)

Umlazi (Black township)
Umuzi (Zulu village)
uSolu (the great African shade tree)
Winterton (town east of the Draco mountains)
Zulu (African language)

✳ ✳ ✳ ✳ ✳ ✳

DISCOVERING NEW LANGUAGES

abaningi amandla - many powers

aikona - no

aloe - plant

amanzi- water

Amphitheatre - sheer rock face atop the Escarpment

Andromeda - galaxy near Milky Way

angaz - don't know

ay - hay

Babloo - chacma baboon's name

bakkie - truck, jeep

Bhaca - African tribe

boer - Farmer

Bomvana - African tribe

Bru - bro, fella

Bulnitramet - fantasy element

bushbucks - type of buck

Busingatha - mountain village

Canis Major - constellation

Carapace - shell

Cathedral Peak - mountain area

chacma - variety of baboon

Colored - bushmen lineage race group in South Africa

Columba the Dove - constellation

domkop-idiot

donga-pothole

drones - mini flying objects

duffel bag-soft bag

Earth-boy hood - hood of Prince Jali'a jacket

ethalion - butterflies

farp - fart

(forest) mother of pearl - butterfly

four-footed butterflies - variety of African butterfly

Goldilocks planet - ideal planet

Halloween-horror celebration

hayibo - wow

Himalayas - oldest mountain range in India

ho - slang for man/guy

Indus - area south of the Himalayas in India

ja - Afrikaans term for yes

jol - party

Ladysmith - town in Kwa-Zulu Natal

laanis - rich people

lammergeyer - vulture

Lepus the Hare - constellation

lungila - I'm well

lutho - nothing

Mfengu - African tribe

mina ay lutho - me, nothing

mina uyo shaya wena - I'll hit you

monkey-thorn tree - pod bearing plant

Mont Aux Sources Hotel - lodge in Draco Mountains

Mpondo - African tribe

Mpondomise - African tribe

muthi - tribal medicine

Mylothris rueppellii - variety of butterfly

Ndebele - African tribe

ooka - yes on Zooka

Orange River - South African river

Orion Nebula - constellation

papyrus-paper on Zooka

Pedi - African tribe

petrol-gas, gasoline

Pondo - African tribe

potjie - cooking vessel

protea - national flower of South Africa

rainbow nation-unity in diversity

reedbuck - mountain buck

sangoma - tribal doctor

San people - ancient bushmen tribe

sand cat - broad faced desert cat

Sentinel - mountain

siya bonga - thank you

smaak - Afrikaans term for like

Sotho - African tribe

Spioenkop - Spy Hill

stinkwood - evergreen tree

strelitzia - bird beaked plant

Swati - African tribe

Thimbu - African tribe

Thukela Falls - highest falls

Thukela Gorge - opening the mountain

Thukela Hut - hut atop the escarpment

Thukela River - South African river

trills - sounds of crickets

Tsonga - African tribe

tussock grass - flora of grasslands

Twsana - African tribe

ubuntu - love, compassion

Ubuntu Circle - circle of love to guard Prince Jali

umnukane - Zulu name for stinkwood tree

umuzi - circular settlement/kraal

uSolu - shade tree

vaai - Indian slang for go

Vaal River - South African river

Venda - African tribe

White Stone - the GIFT

wenzani - what are you doing?

wungani - how are you

Xesbie - African tribe

Xhosa - African language

yebo - yes

yellowwood - coniferous tree

Zulu - African language

✳ ✳ ✳ ✳ ✳ ✳

DrVie.com

My notes